# THE LESBIAN NEXT DOOR

To Warren!

There are no rules for friendship.

—William Hazlitt

Maris Cross Thornton

8.23.01

# THE LESBIAN NEXT DOOR

Mavis Evans

Copyright © 2000 by Mavis Evans.

Library of Congress Number:     00-193299
ISBN #:        Softcover        0-7388-4953-7

All rights reserved. No part of this book may be reproduced or transmitted in any form or by any means, electronic or mechanical, including photocopying, recording, or by any information storage and retrieval system, without permission in writing from the copyright owner.

This is a work of fiction. Names, characters, places and incidents either are the product of the author's imagination or are used fictitiously, and any resemblance to any actual persons, living or dead, events, or locales is entirely coincidental.

This book was printed in the United States of America.

To order additional copies of this book, contact:
Xlibris Corporation
1-888-7-XLIBRIS
www.Xlibris.com
Orders@Xlibris.com

To Gordo

# I

I like square handbags, practical clothes, sensible shoes, organized cupboards, geometric designs, clear colors, and furniture that has withstood the test of time. I don't expect people to live according to my standards. I do expect them to deal as openly and fairly with me as I do with them. I abhor injustice in any form. Trying too hard to do my best, I have been informed, is my worst fault. I could live with that. I liked myself. As Dick Francis, the racehorse author might have put it, this filly was odds-on to run true to form; id est, go the distance, graduate my senior year at college, begin a career in Nutrition Education, make a few compatible contemporary friendships, and get a life other than that of playing the role of only-child, parents-pleaser. Upset comes in the course of the human race when self-styled prognosticators neglect to factor in the one weakness flesh has been heir to since in the Beginning there was Adam and there was Eve.

It happened in October. A split-second eye contact set off a microcosmic tingle between a tall graduate student and my willowy self. He quickly resumed his search for a place to tack his note on the bulletin board on the wall outside the college used book shop. I got on with scanning similarly pinioned paper scraps in the hopes that one advertised an odd job to earn me a few extra bucks. If Marian Evans (George Eliot) admitted in her novel "Middlemarch" a loss for words with which to explain that spontaneous spark between two strangers, other that to say it was the generally accepted mysticism known as falling in love at first sight, who was I to try to define it any better? He needed a typist. I could type. Our romance was off and running.

It all happened too fast. At first I lugged his scribbled compositions and book-marked pages home to Willoughby hills. Commuting saved my parents college dorm fees. During Christmas break I accepted his great grandmother's old gold diamond ring. Cleveland's lake effect snowstorms, plus this token pledge, seemed to make it okay to work and sleep over in John's small, two-room, off-campus apartment. While we abstained from doing 'it', we practised doing everything else but 'it'. Being the personality types we were, a fact that endeared John to me, we decided to get married. Which we did, simply and quietly. The day after I walked across a platform to receive my degree, I walked down the flower-bordered path in my future in-laws' typically English Garden, and exchanged marriage vows beneath a white, vine-entwined arbor. Whom God hath joined, and so forth.

Forthwith, I got a job distantly related to Nutrition Education. My salary was to provide for us while John continued to work full-time towards getting his PhD. To keep expenses down we kept John's hole-in-the-wall apartment. The rhythm method did have something going for it as a means of birth control. Mostly the rhythm; up/down, in/out, really great, then bingo! I got pregnant. I also got the medical advice to stay off my feet or risk losing the baby. Our planned priorities got what we optimistically tagged a slight delay.

Scratch early withdrawal during the sex act. It is only helpful in the cause of family planning if you are planning to have a family. Our second slight delay arrived eleven months after his brother had been born. Early withdrawal became a term only as it applied to our landlady's notice to vacate our wall-to-wall, crib-cramped, living space. My entire neural network went on hold on the rack. John, bless his people talent, handled it. He absolutely agreed with Mrs. Katczymaricvik, and he gave her the courtesy of pronouncing the landlady's name the way she pronounced it with three syllables. He negotiated an extension on our occupancy to enable us to find a larger place. She granted us one month, with the proviso that if a tenant complained about the babies' crying one more time, we were out. Talk about pressure. My theme song became "Hush little baby, don't you cry". Either one of you. Please.

Allow me to introduce myself, and our families, some members of which I may have harmed by what I did it a rash outburst of do-gooder gullibility. Did I do wrong? Did I do right? I need to know, and so I seek reassurance by putting it all down in black and white. Either way, it is a secret I must carry to the grave. I am serious. I am Victorina Saddle. No horse jokes, please. Been there, done that. 'Victorina' after my godfather, my mother's brother, Uncle Victor. We are Italian descent. More, we are Genoese—Genoaysa. These genes make me a blue-eyed blonde.

My husband is John Paul Saddle the Third. It does not signify a papal affiliation. The 'third' does somewhat indicate that he was raised amid comfortable circumstances by a family proud of its lineage. Also, it fit in with the British penchant for the continuing descendant sort of thing. Uppity, his family members are not. Pater-in-law is a lovely, twinkle-in-the-eye sort of chap. My John Paul's social ease no doubt comes from this role model. At first, I judged Mater-in-law to be a wimp. Later, I learned to admire her generous tolerance in the face of what she might refer to as 'little spanners thrown into the works'. Consider what I did to these people when I named their grandsons. It was the first hint of the rebellion a-simmer inside me. I broke the name chain. Number one son was Benjamin Alister. Robert Dennison was son number two's monicker. Monicker, indeed, because these impressive names quickly Damon Runyonesqu-ed to

Benny and Bobby. Nonetheless, their paternal grandfather's comment was a 'Bully for you, Victorina', and John's mother accepted the names as 'good' names for our little men. Her other most frequently used adjective was 'nice'. Everything to her was either 'good' or 'nice' Sometimes, 'quite nice'. These expressions were the evidence for my early judgement of her as a wimp.

Thwarted, thereby, in this rebel need to shock, I decided that I could not stick staunchly to credos if I could not buy the whole kit and kaboodle. Following the birth of two sons in two years, I allowed my non-practising Episcopalian (Anglican to the Saddles), to practise a more foolproof birth control. In fact, I insisted upon it. No argument from a supportive John. Retrospect tells me that I skipped a life-stage, the stage when in early adulthood I should have had the chance to feel free and independent. One school of psychological thought states that a stage skipped, is a stage often lived out of sequence. Not an excuse, but maybe a reason for the sudden urge to liberate myself from such restrictions as the narrowing of the female mind by root-bound catholicism. Invisible chains bound me in wifehood and motherhood. Duty ruled, but it chafed something awful.

John' sister rubbed me the wrong way. Thin, her angularity echoed in her sharp intelligence, it would be politically correct to describe her as sobriety challenged. I now blush at my scorn for her. I didn't know then that inherited traits foster behaviors that some people are forced to contend with for every waking hour for all the days of their lives; allergies, adictive tendencies, and other ways in which God made them different.

If Ma noticed any difference in her only chick, she was not talking about it.. This difference had manifested itself after I had gotten married, ergo, it might connote sexual overtones. This was the one and only subject upon which Ma would not express her verbal opinions. At top volume. Who can imagine their parents having sex? Not I. Ma and Pa must have had sex once, at least, for here was I, but vent their passion in loud arguments, they did. I vowed that John and I would never ever yell at each other the way my parents did. We would discuss our differences of opinions calmly. If he ever finds out what I did, reading me the riot act will be his least punishment. More shame to me, I am not sorry for what I did, only confused about ethics. Oh to return to the time when our only problem was to find a house before Mrs. Katczymaricvik kicked us out onto the street, or worse, we were forced to move in with either set of parents!

# II

First, we had to find some money. John's trust fund, left to him by his grandmother, showed a six thousand and ten dollar balance. Our joint savings account contained seven hundred and thirteen bucks. John sold his motorcycle. Sacrificed it, is a more accurate term. No moans, but I recognized a stiff upper lip when I saw it. FHA mortgage loans required a ten percent down payment. At that rate we figured we could afford a house in the seventy-five thousand dollar price range.

We revealed as much to Claire, the realtor. She deserved an Academy Award for her outward composure when she learned the bottom-line max we could afford to get ourselves into a house. She actually smiled. Spoke encouraging words.

"I do have a couple of houses listed that might interest you. That is, if you're not afraid of doing a bit of hard work."

The two vacant houses Claire drove us to see stood shoulder to shoulder in close order file with their occupied neighbors along a one-sided street. Although set back by virtue of a marginal route and an unkempt weedy area edging a six-foot high, protective, wire fence, these old houses did face the freeway. They occupied a no-man's land, not exactly within the city proper, and not far out enough to be considered in the suburbs.

They bore a sameness in that they were all more than fifty years old. Unlike the sameness found in suburban developments where the attempts to promote individualistic styling ran to door and and window selections, these houses were totally unique as to size, shape, and the building materials used. Claire confided that these houses had personalities, and that a prospective buyer had to recognize this charm about them, to be able to envision their potential. Plus the big plus, they sold for well below the market value. They represented a profit to be made, especially if they were restored to tip-top condition.

A big if, indeed. Renovations cost. The first house we approached sported a high-pitched roof, the inverted 'V' of it to the left and right sides, the long slants of it to the front and rear. Two pairs of oxeye dormer windows projected two by two, one pair in the front of the long slant, the other pair in the rear. So positioned, they gave any occupant a view of the street, or a look at the backyard. It also had windows in the side walls, a feature modern houses seem to lack. The better to be neighborly?

The amateur repairs inflicted upon the exterior served only to accent its state of disrepair. A previous owner had shingled over the porch railing spindles with the shingles left over from the vile green items overlapping in eroded rows atop the roof. A homemade wooden sign, atilt to starboard on its one pegleg, faintly proclaimed 'For Sale' amid a wild sea of tangled grasses. Taking advantage of our polite failure to comment on the plight of this poor orphan, Clair waggled a dungeoner's key in the front door's rusty lock until the springbolt surrendered and gave access to interior gloom.

Nothing daunted, Claire switched on the bare bulb dangling over the hallway beyond the front door, and proceeded to point out the house's unusual floor plan. A kitchen and a diningroom split by entrance hallway occupied the front section of the house. Very unusual placement, Claire informed us, a kitchen at the front of a house. Two Lilliputian bedrooms, kept apart by a narrow bathroom, claimed the remaining space to the rear. So far, so bad, except the house had an endearing feature to me. Its attic immediately beneath that tented roof. The dormer windows and the roof's lofty peak gave this spacious area headroom. The studs stood bare, but the walls they fronted at intervals were birdseye maple, and the never-sanded planked oak floor whispered plenty of potential hiding beneath its dusty mantle. What a great dormitory for Benny and Bobby!

What finally sold us on the poor orphan's neighbor, despite a heavier mortgage, was the fact that it was in better condition. The roof was new enough that it was still watertight. It had the potential for a family room addition behind the back kitchen. And, and, and! It had these sort of plaster Corinthian pillars between the token front parlor and the large diningroom thusly separated from it. Lives there a romanticist who could resist classically scrolled, pseudo-Greek pillars? The ten-foot ceilings appealed to my six-foot-three husband, the first floor soar having been a steal from the three bedrooms upstairs. I figured, low ceilings, so what? People were usually horizontal in bedrooms, weren't they? We were sold.

Claire stood by us through negotiation to a rock-bottom asking price, and figuratively held our hands during the rigmarole of signing away our meagre savings account, into which, the future held no possibility of further deposits, because a frighteningly large chunk of our single income would go straight to the bank in monthly mortgage installments. The deed transfer was a done deal by the end of May. It had taken up more time than our one month grace period. Mrs. K. was on the point of taking legal action to evict us. Once again, John segued into her good graces by taking advantage of her weak spot. He told her she could keep his first two months' advance payment that he had paid when he first rented the apartment—if she let us hang in for a just another week or so.

We moved out the second week in June. It seemed expedient to leave everything but the bare necessities in cartons until cleaning and a plan for general repairs and renovation could be drawn up. A big mistake. Living out of boxes and suitcases was strictly for the birds. However, that tacit agreement that lay between John and me as to how, and by whom, these alterations, etcetera, would be accomplished needed to be be more explicit for we two professional people, the better to avoid future arguments. We made out two lists; His and Hers.

An east-side community college had hired John to teach English Literature and to direct the fund-raising theatrical entertainment put on in the auditorium twice a year. He was free from classes (and paycheck) until mid-july, at which time he would take on a lighter load of two summer courses and some extracurricular tutorial work for a few struggling students. Extra money. All of which would go for groceries and the dreaded mortgage hanging over our heads. We decided in team effort that John's prime concern should be to get the family room addition roughed out to the point that it could be enclosed before the cold weather set in. What with his academic responsibilities eased off, John felt that he had plenty of time to accomplish this definitely male task. He liked to exude a male aura, as he half-believed that teaching drama might label him as a bit 'fruity'. As his bed partner, I can guarantee he definitely was not. The operative words here 'plenty of time' and 'no problem'.

As household upgrade befitting the female half of the team, I would paint the kitchen cabinets inside and out, they badly needed it, and the kitchen chores definitely defined the woman's bailiwick. Bit by bit when time permitted, I could strip wallpaper layers from the diningroom and the parlor plaster-and-lath multi-papered over perimeters. Plus, a few inches, in any free moments, by easy stages, sand the handrail atop the classically influenced balusters. (an attempt to to match the Corinthian pillars?) Remove the cracked varnish in easy steps, at my leisure. Between child care, meals, and the proliferative laundry loads.

We got off to a good start. Uncle Victor's construction company sent out a digger thingie and a concrete mixer truck. John helped the men get the earth moved and the footers poured mostly by supplying them with coffee, cold beer, or colas on demand. The family room would have to be two steps down from the kitchen. I liked it. Aesthetically pleasing. The boys were happy to sit in their highchairs with traysful of Cheerios or cut-up fruit bits and stare with fascination at the rumbling machinery. I got one whole kitchen cupboard painted that week. Well, perking the coffee, sugaring and creaming it to individual tastes, and handing out cans of beer or cola to John to hand to the laborers did take time. That's one whole cupboard, inside and out. John commented on the neat job I was doing.

Ma and Pa had given us a range and a refrigerator as a housewarming present. Mater and Pater Saddle, not to be outdone, and fair up to their typically English teeth, donated a washer and a dryer to the cause. Maxed to its limit, our Visa card bought us, thanks to Uncle Victor's discounted price, the boards, planks, screws and two-by-fours to build the family room above the concrete footer—Uncle Victor's contribution to the cause. The Visa payments were low enough if one didn't think about the interest added each month to the balance owing. I economized by buying a playpen at a garage sale. Benny and Bobby could play safely therein, and watch their mother strip and sand. All systems were go.

Before too many nails bit into the boards, John had to go do his duty at the college. As the summer wore on I began to wonder what was wrong with me. I had it all; a husband teaching at a college, working towards a PhD with subsequent promotions and a bright future in view. Two bright sons. And a house to raise them in. What was the matter with me?

The house was the matter with me. I had to stay in that house. Day after day. Cleaning, cooking, caring for children, children at an age when they needed constant supervision, myself lonely for adult company. Disappointed at a hard-won career as a professional nutritionist terminated by pregnancy after a few months on the job. A one-car budget strained to its limits. Housebound with a boring daily routine overload. John sympathized with one ear, and heard the call of urgent necessity with the other. The need to finish his education. To complete his thesis. To do the best job he could at the college so that his resumé would be a beneficial document when seeking a higher paying position. What more could he do when even ordering in a pizza was a major expense? We were a one-income family in a two-income economy. We were determined to be independent. We were strapped for money because we had invested in a fixer upper to turn into our dream house. We had bitten off more than we could chew. The house had turned into a nightmare that had turned on us. It had us drowning in debt right up to my baby blues eyeballs.

If ever there was a misnomer, the word 'playpen' is it. Benny was a toddler. Toddlers crave, yearn, and ache to toddle. He sounded in agony in the playpen. When lifted into it he set his little chin above the rail, stuck out his lower lip, and when that didn't work, opened his mouth in roars of protest. Bobby, ever struggling to imitate his big brother, failed to pull himself to his feet, but cried as loudly in earsplitting disharmony. Older people say that they remember exactly what they were doing when J.F. Kennedy was shot. I was too young to remember the assassination, but I do remember exactly what I was doing on one particular day. The day of the ultimate playpen rebellion.

I was stripping wallpaper. Unstuck wallpaper webbed my fingers and clung to the diningroom walls as resolutely as any vines at Oxford. The din and mess was too much. I stopped working. Reconnoitered my accomplishments to date. Two kitchen cabinets enamelled. Six inches of bared oak showing on the stair bannister. Almost all of an eighteen inch wide strip, removed through five layers down to bare plaster, as far down as the chair rail. All the toys had made the flight out of the playpen, and the return toss, at least a dozen times. Plastic sheets flapped ineffectually around the family room studding. It was September, growing colder, and there was no way that John was going to nail up outside walls, teach, and write before the snow fell. The color of my post-natal despondency suddenly deepened from baby blues to Holly Golightly's mean reds. We were in the red. The fumes from chemical stripping compounds had bloodshot the whites of my eyes. cuticles bled red. A raw roast of beef looked better than my sore, swollen hands. The blues and reds of my emotions churned together until a purple rage held me in its grip. If you can't lick 'em, join 'em. I climbed into the playpen. Squatted, long legs akimbo. Hugged my wailing babies and howled along with them. This I remember because my Uncle Victor chose that moment to walk in unannounced. He made me an offer we couldn't refuse. His offer, although he did not say so, entailed the introduction of homosexuality into our home. When John found out, later, it provoked a Ma and Pa shouting type of argument that I had vowed never to let happen in our marriage.

Uncle Victor had taken one look at my hands as he held them to haul me up out of the playpen.

"Cara mia! This is too much! I have two men who need to be kept busy since we are almost finished a big job. They will be glad to come over and help you.

## III

The two men arrived, not so much glad as willing. For their boss's relative, they were willing workers. They waited in their open bed truck until John backed off the short driveway fronting our detached one-car garage, and then pulled in to take his place. Their thick-soled work boots tramped across the lawn (using the term loosely) patch to meet the children and me on the front porch, from where we had waved goodbye to Daddy. Derek introduced himself and presented the second man as Sime. I later learned that Sime was short for Simon.

Derek was built like a construction worker. Broad shoulders, muscular arms, sleeves rolled up, narrow waist, and regarding him from a professional standpoint, I would say he was a well-nourished young man. About three years younger than my twenty-seven years. Sime must have been in his forties. I based this assumption on the cords in his neck, the sinews in his skinny arms, minimum grey strands in his lank black hair, and sunken cheeks which exaggerated his beaky nose. Bony fingers raked his hair back and waggled around as if they couldn't stay still, but they never touched the unlit cigarette stuck between his thin lips. A funny thing, that. His tongue and lips could move that cigarette from side to side, Sime could even talk around it, take cola or beer swig, and it never fell out.

He couldn't be accused of smoking, but in my estimation a change in his dietary habits would do him a lot of good.

Ruff-Ruff, our Jack Russell terrier, a low to the ground, long-bodied, square-jawed protector, determined to protect us, uttered a warning growl. Derek squatted down to the dog's level and persuaded Ruff-Ruff via voice and ear scratches that he and Sime meant no harm. Sime's cigarette did not seem in the least convinced that Ruff-Ruff meant no harm, either. It vibrated in a trembly fashion while the men sized up the job to be done. I offered to brew fresh coffee. Derek turned it down, saying that they only had until noon that day to get a jump on what had to be done here. He looked at his partner for confirmation. Sime's cigarette twitched a sharp jerk up down. Derek translated.

"You three would be a big help if you took the dog for a walk."

I got the message. "A long walk?"

Derek smiled his approval. Bright teeth dazzled. The dazzle remained in an after image, but Ruff-Ruff's leash got attached to the double stroller, Bobby sat strapped into it, Benny helped push it, his mother's hand keeping a guiding grip on the stroller's handle—both to synchronize the forward propellers, and to act as a brake. The shadow of Derek's smile kept me company. I blew the illusion away on an exhaled sigh. A married woman with two children had no business drooling over young male hunks. What was the matter with me? Maybe the problem stemmed from the no-fun slavery John and I had put in all summer. Beware the fixer upper. It will lure in with its lower mortgage crocodile smile, then wholly swallow your time and energy in greedy sequential gulps. Rending heart and soul. Painfully wearying. I shuddered at how close John and I had come to following sharp retorts with vociferous arguments. Since Derek and Sime had respectively smiled and waved a cigarette goodbye to release me from the manual labor arena, I made a mental promise to fix John a special dinner, and a calmer, well-groomed wife to meet him when he got home. For the first time in a month I smiled to myself at that good idea. John had worked hard, too, and deserved a pleasant surprise.

We had reached the west end of our street of older homes and estimable trees. Summer was holding its own, but fall infiltrated in artful ways. Here a leaf had changed to a warmer color, there a ripe nut sprinkle, everywhere brisk fresh air whisked away the cloying remnants of sticky humidity that August had left behind. The street remained deserted. Spooky to be the sole souls abroad, but it seemed safe enough, especially with Ruff-Ruff on guard. Around a corner, and further progress, brought us to a small neighborhood store. Bobby, writhing to free himself from his stroller harness, needed distraction. An oriental shopkeeper held the door open for us. He shook his head in a slight objection to the dog, but I said we just wanted Oreos and jellybeans real quick, if he had them. He did, and slippered away to get them from shelf and candy jar. Some nutritionist! Rescued my professional side with a so what! We deserved a treat and time off for good behavior.

Another block down I could see the elementary school that the boys might attend in the future. We headed for it with our goodies. No pupils were about. school had not reconvened for the fall term. Labor Day was still the deadline for summer's end and back to school, then. The play yard was ours for the taking. Bobby sat on my lap nibbling an Oreo cookie while my right foot toes pressed into the bare earth pushed our swing back and forth. Benny made for the geodesic dome climber. He struggled every whichaway to get either little toddler leg over the lowest metal pipes. He ran around and around the metal monster seeking purchase. Grasped at bars as high up as his little arms could reach. Wore himself out. I didn't help him as I remembered a lesson from an early childhood development course; a child will climb only as high on anything as he can manage to climb down from. Parents or sitters who help with a boost are interfering with a child's unfolding ability to to form physical, spatial judgements. It was hard not to run to Benny's aid, especially when his frustration turned vocal.

I rose from the swing, Bobby lost a lap so I carefully set him on his feet. He could maintain his balance and stagger along if someone held both his hands. I called to Benny that Bobby and I were going over to the schoolyard fence to pick some of the flowers blooming among the weeds that were tough enough to survive along the wire boundary. Benny hesitated. I told him that the pink flowers would make the dinner table pretty for Daddy. We needed his help, please. It was a try to give him a way out of the geodesic dome puzzle without leaving him with a sense of failure. I hoped. He finally toddled over. The flowers came off more easily than the stems which were woody. Maybe displaced wood anemones? I accepted the plucked blooms gratefully. Tiny flowerets afloat it a glass bowl would look very nice on the table. 'Nice'? I was beginning to sound like my mother-in-law. I decided it was time to head for home.

Neither son put up a fuss at riding in the double stroller for the return trip. Chewy jellybeans doled out for the occasion kept them busy. Ruff-Ruff was panting from thirst and straining at his leash. We had been away from home for over two hours. I followed Ruff-Ruff's lead and upped the pace. I rounded the corner going full tilt. I was in time to see a man and two women checking out the house next door to us. At this distance I assumed that trio consisted of a husband and wife, and a real estate agent, although the agent was not Claire. Claire's silhouette would have projected a larger bosom. A silent prayer was added to the homeward rush. Let these house hunters appreciate the potential of the Attic loft. Let the woman be a stay-at-home housewife. Let her like children. Let her be close enough to my age to be a close friend. No warning thought reminded me of the embroidered sampler hanging inside a frame on Ma and Pa's bedroom wall.

'be careful what you pray for, you might get it'

Inside my own front door a surprise awaited. Both the handrail and the steps to the second floor had been sanded to pristine condition. Totally prepared to be stained and varnished. The spontaneous delighted expression on my face evoked another perfect smile from Derek. He was gathering up his tools, but he assured me than Sime and he would be back the next day. The bunch of us traipsed into the kitchen just as Sime, as nimble as any tree swinger, swung down from the slope of the boarded and tarpapered roof. We all trooped in cautious foot placement across the unfinished family room horizontal two-by-fours, descended the makeshift cement block steps to admire Sime's work from the backyard. Sime's cigarette wig-wagged a signal to Derek, then drooped at the sight of Ruff-Ruff. I got a grip on the dog's leash still attached to his collar and exclaimed at how quickly he had gotten the roof ready for the shingles. The droopy cigarette took and upward turn for the better. Even seemed to manage a self-satisfied goodbye twitch.

Benny and Bobby were more eager to say hello to their bottles than to finish their cut-up grilled cheese sandwiches. The jellybeans had taken the edge of their appetites. They climbed up the smoothed steps on their hands and feet, their mother following behind in case the climbing theory had a flaw in it, eight ounces of juice in nippled bottles in either hand. I paused halfway up the stairs where a porthole window kept a glass eye on the house next door. The one-legged sign was in the same position as we would be in very shortly; flat on its back. Puns get a bad rap, but mine gave me a smile. That was a good sign!

For once, the boys went down for their naps as gently as little lambs. Showered, terry robe clad, I spread out in comfort beneath the comforter on the master bedroom bed, with the intention to follow Sue Grafton's poking and prying technique towards solving a murder mystery. It never happened. Into the land of instant snooze was I as speedily as if I was doing one of her runs she purportedly does to keep in shape.

Rested, eager to tell about our day, Benny, Bobby and I waited at the door to welcome Daddy home. John entered traffic tensed, a strained patience in his 'Hi Guys' greeting to his sons, an attitude that came across as a bit of a resentment that we presented him with cheerful and happy while he felt browned off and beat. He came to the kitchen table twenty minutes later, withdrawn and quiet, his body language giving away that he was still in the same frame of mind. We reacted naturally. We all wanted Daddy to feel happy with us. We learned that sometimes people who feel unhappy, don't want to be made to feel happy.

Benny drew John's attention to the 'fowahs'. John relented enough to admit they looked nice on the table. ('nice' inherited?) Then took the shine off his compliment by asking me if flower picking was a good activity for the boys? Implication, too namby-pamby? To change the subject, I drew his attention to the family room progress. The fact that Uncle Victor had sent two men to usurp his place as man-of-the-house renovator hit him squarely in his own masculinity. Did Uncle Victor think that he couldn't get the job done? Overt anger accompanied the thought that I had let two strange men into the house while his wife and children were alone. It did no good to explain that the men were not exactly strange—well, Sime was a tad strange—not strangers. Uncle Victor knew them. A try to lighten the darkness— Ruff-Ruff might be small but he was a dog to be reckoned with. Bred by an English clergyman to hunt large rodents, a go for the throat of any foe inherent in them, Jack Russell terriers were capable of five-foot, vertical leaps upwards, from a standing start. Iron-grip jaws. Ruff-Ruff would have protected us against any invader. John didn't want to hear it.

A subdued quiet reigned. I introduced a less controversial subject.

"I think the house next door was sold today."

John scowled. Tossed down his napkin to challenge, "That's just great! You know what kind of people probably bought that dump? (Like us? crossed my mind) People down on their luck! Pains in the neck with a bunch of undisciplined kids who will be all over the place. Their parents dashing over here to borrow stuff. Or steal it. Don't you go getting too darned neighborly with them."

John said he was sorry at bedtime. I cut him some slack. It wasn't his habit to dump on us. Usually, he supported me in my rollercoaster mood swings of late. He agreed that the family room did need to be enclosed before the snow fell. He could rearrange his schedule to help Uncle Victor's men on the weekends. At least until it was time to rehearse the students who were acting the roles in the Christmas play fund-raiser. He could neglect his thesis for a couple of weeks and work on the repairs in the evenings. And, yeah, the men hadn't been unknown quantities. Which reminded him of those other unknown quantities.

"But", and here John raised himself up onto his elbow for emphasis, "I don't want those new neighbors on a run-in-and-out basis. I know you. You will let them take advantage of you. I am serious about this, Vickie."

To prove it, he got down off his elbow, got serious, and took advantage of me. I let him.

# IV

So, of course, around the first of October, while the sweater-clad boys, Ruff-Ruff and I walked the streets to be out from underfoot, and to keep the great white unlit cigarette at a work perky angle, when a white Mustang nosed into the curb, and a moving van humped its trailer onto the driveway of the house next door, what should we exiles do but trot over en masse to see if we could help in any way. We could. Right off the bat these new neighbors needed to borrow something. John's warnings niggled, but my natural bent to be a good Samaritan took care of them. Besides, who would be so callous as to deny that vivacious, smiling, curly-headed brunette the loan of a cup of sugar or some such trivial thing? Or anything she needed, for that matter.

Actually, it was her roofer who needed to borrow our electricity to be able to use his power tools. He had my consent even before he made me an offer only an idiot would refuse. His company would pay my utility bill for the entire month. Delilah Sealman introduced herself and thanked me profusely all in one breath. On her next breath she explained that she and Les wanted to reshingle the whole roof. They didn't want any more water stains on a really neat floor in the attic. She giggled. And wasn't the color so awful? It looked as if the house had gall bladder problems. She gave me no chance to get a word in edgewise. She excused herself on the grounds that she had a gadzillion things to do, took the time before she whirled away to wave to Benny and Bobby parked in their double stroller. Those traitors struggled to escape in an attempt to follow her to the ends of the earth. Or into her house. Whichever came first.

We pushed for home. My mind dwelt on Delilah Sealman. Delilah had recognized the loft's potential. Her wave to the children showed a liking for children. She was close enough to my age to be a close friend. Yes, yes, and yes. Observations on three commonalities encouraging enough to give her the status of being a front runner in the soulmate department. Yes!

Suddenly, the autumn sun came out. Foliage tapestries radiated a new brilliance, reminded me that the leaves on our front grass patch needed to be raked together. As fast as the piles grew, Benny and Bobby dove into them. I pretended dismay. They squealed their delight. Ruff-Ruff, tethered to the maple tree trunk, got his exercise that day from his leaps and barks at the end of his rope. Okay. So it was a sneaky ploy to keep an eye on the house next door until Derek and Sime packed it in and we could go indoors for lunch.

These men tidied up after themselves. The renovations went on apace with nary a planed wood curl, a grain of sawdust, or a bent nail left in evidence at day's end. It paid to have a relative in the construction business, thought I. Uncle Victor not only donated his men, he also got the materials wholesale for us. John and Derek teamed up for the next few weekends. Sime must have had other unsmoked fish to fry. Too bad, because his Twiggy-type arms slung four-by-eight plywood flooring off the truck bed as easily as if they had been cardboard. Who cared if the extent of his vocabulary varied between grunted huffs and a nicotine-free puff? He had that family room floor laid and waiting for the cheapest synthetic carpet we could find to cover it up, and only one wall still displayed studs uncovered by wallboard. Still, lacking Sime on the job, John and Derek worked well together.

Except that John was hard put to keep up with Derek in the sheer physical energy it took to scrape, paint, and climb ladders to restore the exterior redwood siding. October proved unseasonably hot that fall. The two males worked stripped to the waist. John looked flab-free and in fairly trim shape. Derek's body showed off abs and pecs from what had to be a combination of physical labor and Olympic-class workouts. It was evident in the efforts John exerted to keep up with his fellow painter, that he had noticed Derek's splendid musculature. At day's end, John looked so bushed as Derek gaily smiled and waved his way out of our driveway. I tried bucking him up with a compliment.

"The house looks great. You sure chose the right color when you insisted on the Williamsburg grey. Aren't you glad we didn't go with that plastic siding stuff? When the black shutters go up I'll love it."

The shutters were synthetic. They are the cheapest way to spruce up an exterior decor. John accepted the praise with a squeeze from a tired arm laid across my shoulders. It lacked the strength to dispel the unease I sensed in John's sense of his own machismo. Especially when he begged this question.

"Did you get a load of the build on that guy?"

Some lesser god stifled an immediate impulse to respond, "Yeah, Baby! Like Wow!" Warned that exclamations to an exhausted husband in comparison to a hunk's build was a definite no-no. A half truth seemed preferable to no truth at all. I gave him a vague reply that I really hadn't gotten a really good look at the man. I had been too busy with the children. Moved right along to ask my hero what he would like for dinner. The choices were meatloaf and mashed potatoes, or spaghetti and the meat made into balls. By that time I had learned fifty different ways to disguise hamburger. John's sense of humor returned at the description of the same meat made into balls. He gave his wife a whole-hearted hug and told me to surprise him. I nestled into his embrace and warned him not to tempt me. He eyed me as if giving that some thought. I thought, case of the carpenter competition closed. I should have added, "Not!"

Uncle Victor, a long-time widower, his young wife having died before their first anniversary, absolutely lived to latch onto every set of circumstances that promoted a family celebration. The family room rated a grand opening. November thrummed its rainy days prelude to old man winter, and Ma's brother was voicing the lyrics she relished above all others; let's all get together and eat. Ma baked a lasagna that Napoleon's army could have travelled on all the way to Moscow. Uncle Victor donated vintage Asti Spumonti. Benny and Bobby had licked residual frosting from bowls and spoons in the process of their mother's chocolate cupcake preparations. Mother-in-law Saddle did better than cook. To the feast she brought gourmet-level cold cuts, exotic cheeses, veggies crudité, the lot arranged artistically on trays by a parsley-savvy chef. John had strung a red paper ribbon across the arched opening between the kitchen and the family room.

The festivities began with Grandfather Saddle's hand cupping Benny's hold on the children's blunt-nosed scissors. A few wobbles and bobbles, and snip/snip/snip parted the red tape to complete the ceremony. We all cheered and chowed down to serious eating, serving ourselves onto styrofoam plates from the kitchen counter 'buffet'. Somehow, everyone found places among our few chairs, meagre furniture, and the as yet, unpacked cardboard cartons. Father-in-law Saddle gallantly leaned against a wall to leave seating opportunities for the ladies. Our over-hearty indulgences eventually gave way to small talk. Wine loosens tongues.

Mater Saddle adjudged Uncle Victor's Asti Spumonti to be very 'nice', indeed. Coming from this lady, 'very nice' was high praise. Calm and composed was her style. How different from my own Ma who often hit the excitability charts on a scale close to ten. Her most often repeated phrases that day, after each renovation inspection, began to dampen the spirit in which the party was given.

Examples: "What's the matter with you?" and "Are you crazy?" "Why do you gotta waste so much money on such a (I think the word she used from the Genoese meant) bummer!" More in varied critique, but the same in tone.

It is a fallacy abroad, I think, that Italian men are kings of their own affairs. In my family, my father always consulted with, and sought his wife's advice when it came to business and money. And he got plenty of it. Advice, not money. Her message, though unasked for, read that the outlay cost too much for investment in the district in which the house was located. She direly predicted never would we recoup our losses.

John, ever the soother, innocent and uninformed on this aspect of Ma's pessimism where spending money was concerned, patiently strove to explain that money put into real estate was better than putting money in the bank. That real estate always increased in value.

"What real estate? You call this real estate? A junk heap next door to you? Just who do you think will come along to waste money on that eyesore?"

John had her there for a few moments. In his persuasive director's voice, used to elicit the best performances from students trying to act in plays, he politely tried to allay her fears. Why, the house next door was sold. He had seen the husband reshingling the roof. It was going to be fine. Not to worry.

Ma was having none of that. The wine in her insisted that that in her own words,

"No matter how much money they pour into that dump, or how hard they work on it, no good will come from those neighbors next door! That is my last word on the subject!"

Lest it wasn't, I changed the subject. I reminded Ma of how generous Uncle Victor (her beloved 'baby' brother, in that he was ten years her junior) had been in getting us stuff wholesale, and how very much we appreciated the help from Sime and Derek—at his expense. Promoted, to all and sundry, that Derek was a really good guy. I didn't know that 'guy' is now considered a generic noun, and can designate whether a male or female or whatever. It turned out that I was using it correctly in that instance.

I had to say, Derek was a peach. He not only scraped, hammered and varnished, he toted in those thick, heavy, sample books so that I could choose wallcoverings for the diningroom and the little parlor. I sang praises for his knowledge of alternatives to plain old wallpaper; lincrusta, for example. How he seemed to feel exactly the effect I was aiming for. Uncle Victor tossed in a conversational bombshell.

"So why shouldn't he? He is almost a woman himself."

John's eyebrows performed a Gothic arches shot upwards.

Uncle Victor laughed at his reaction. "Don't look so surprised. You had to see the guy is gay."

Mater Saddle caught that remark, murmured, "How nice. Noel Coward was referred to quite often as a gay person. He wrote very good plays. Gay sort of romps, and all that. I must say I enjoyed them."

John beat an immediate retreat to the backyard. Father Saddle winked at me. No one present seemed inclined to disillusion his fair lady. Actually, no one seemed to know what to say, and since the host had departed the company abruptly, the company shortly departed the host.

# V

The mood at the breakfast table often sends signals as to how the rest of the day will go. John had sat up half the night on our dilapidated, apartment-days couch, watching old movies on t.v. in our now-habitable, to-a-degree, family room. His Monday morning mood was anyone's guess, so I concentrated on the children. As young as they were they were forming lifelong eating habits. I had received accolades for my final paper in Nutrition Education. Its subject theorized ways in which to influence, positively, children's attitudes towards foods. One behavior modification suggested allowing a child to choose foods from the supermarket shelves, and to let him help prepare part of his meals. I tried to practise what I had preached.

Bobby had picked up a box of Cheerios on our last shopping expedition. He was busy improving his thumb/index finger dexterity by picking up individual O's from his highchair tray. An occasional circlet went into his mouth. More got experimentally dropped over the tray's edge onto the floor. Ruff-Ruff approved my laissez-faire method of child feeding. The Jack Russell's attitude towards table foods rated high marks. When it came to commercial dog food, he definitely had an attitude problem. One sniff turned him off the wet canned stuff. Dry kernels went ker-spit. I had decided that he wouldn't starve as long as Benny and Bobby were around.

Benny had helped stir cream of wheat (his choice at the store) and water into his plastic cereal bowl. He sat waiting for the microwave oven to go 'beep'. Enter John Paul the third looking all spiffy for his day in the classroom. I tried not to envy him. I poured him a cup of coffee and pushed the toaster lever down. Toast and coffee was all John ever ate for breakfast, the most important meal of the day. No amount of educating or coercion did a bit of good; you are setting a bad example for your sons, for example. His attitudes had been set in concrete long ago. On the bright side, if ever a chance arose to sleep late, he was capable of making his own breakfast. I contented myself with using whole wheat bread for the toast. His mother probably would have said—a compromise, that's nice.

The microwave went 'beep'. I tested the cream of wheat for temperature and set it before Benny. He resumed stirring it. I showed his how to spoon it up and pretended to put it in my mouth. He spooned some cereal up, not too carefully, and thrust the loaded spoon towards me. I tried to guide it back towards his mouth. He struggled. The food missed his mouth and splattered onto the highchair tray. John's spoon, over-stirring his coffee, betrayed an irritated stirrer. I thought that he was upset with Benny. I shot him a warning, not-to-tease glance. He shot back,

"Can you believe that guy?"

Benny needed my help. Thus, my, "What guy?' was an automatic reflex rather than a question denoting any real interest in whatever guy he was talking about.

"C'mon. You know darned well just what guy!"

I wiped Benny's chin. "Oh. You mean Derek? It has nothing to do with us."

John was not to be put off his subject. He went on at great length about that guy managing to pass himself as straight. How the guy had fooled him into working cheek-by-jowl with a-a-"

Helpfully meant, "A homosexual?"

Helpful, it was not. John's spoon rattled onto the table. Benny tuned in to see such fun. John had upped his volume to accuse that guy of stripping off his shirt on purpose, just to show off his muscles. Offended masculinity? Threatened masculinity? It crossed my mind that John thought Derek was giving him a come-on. Reinforced this suspicion.

"And to think he had the nerve to pat me on the back and put his arms around me, pretending to be happy about the job being done!" (I had seen this as hail-fellow well-done reciprocal)

It was too much for Benny. He wanted his mother's attention returned to him. He dumped his whole bowl of cream of wheat in kitchen floor bombardment. Ruff-Ruff quickly had that mess under control. John needed my attention more that Benny. Unfortunately, his exaggerated vexation at having been maybe approached for sexual favors aroused my sense of humor. I was laughing so hard that I fully expected my next words to be received in the spirit in which they were given.

One shoulder lifted flirtatiously, "So you were admiring a gay guy's torso, you rascal you!"

John got to his feet. His chair lost its balance and tipped over. "And don't use that word in front of the kids!"

How stupid could I get? I had to ask, "What word? Gay? Get a grip. Do you mean to tell me there has never been a gay young man in your drama classes?"

"Never! I would have spotted it right away!"

My first retaliative retort ran along the lines—if you are so smart, why didn't you see that Derek was gay?—got rejected in favor of a lesser charge.

"Oh yeah! What about that lightfooted fellow who played Puck in 'A Midsummer Night's Dream' that you directed when we were in college? Pr-e-e-e-ty fay, if you ask me."

"Of course he looked fay. He was playing the part of a fairy!"

Why hadn't I quit while he was ahead? I don't know. I couldn't resist this bit of teasing, "And rather well, too. Type casting?"

John struggled against laughter, was about to give in to the impulse when Benny began banging his spoon and chanting, "Day . . . Day . . . Day . . ."

John easily translated it to Gay, Gay, Gay. "Now see what you've done! I don't want your Uncle Victor to send that guy over here ever again. Do you hear me? You tell him that!"

A little 'why me?' crept in, enough for me to take a stand. "Loud and clear. But not until after today. Derek's bringing over a binder full of lincrusta samples. He thinks I would like it below the dado strip in the parlor."

Sure stumped John. "Lincrusta? What's that?"

Glad to be interfacing on a calmer level, "It's a textured wall covering, sort of old-fashioned. It will fit in with our pillars." Never did know when to shut up. "You know—uh-Derek's kind of—well, the Arts have a lot of—look at Somerset Maugham—Rock Hudson—. I don't think they could help being that way." Barged right into another big mistake. "Any family could have a homosexual born into it."

Ma and Pa had nothing on us. John absolutely roared, "Not in this family!"

Benny wanted in on this. He had been fingerpainting with the cream of wheat mush smeared on his highchair tray. He began to shriek, "See! Benny make pitty. See Mama!"

John turned up the heat. "Hear that? You're encouraging him!"

Had I missed a beat? "Encouraging hime? Encouraging him in what? Being artistic?"

Bobby joined the fracas to scream for his 'bah-bah'. In a ballet level movement I twirled in a valiant attempt to halt Benny's splashing hands with one of mine, confirmed his smudges to be pretty, at the same time making a pass at giving Bobby his bottle of orange juice from the counter. A stretch, but I made it. John was not making it.

"Why is that kid still sucking on a bottle? You're making him into a sissy!"

I extemporized. A fancy way to cover my lie. A first lie in our marriage. That first lie carried back-breaking guilt. All subsequent fibs yielded painlessly to rationalization.

Original prevarication, "I'm not supposed to put Bobby on cup until he has-has mastered progressive swallowing. Dr. Schwartz said I should wait for signs of that."

The rationalization: Dear God, it was so lovely to put the boys down for their afternoon naps, each with the comfort of a bottle. No crying. A two-hour respite for me. My only break from being on call twenty-four hours a day, seven days a week. A time to reap hot bathtub soaks. A time to be comforted. Per-chance to knitteth up the ravelled sleeve of care. All unwittingly, I had formed a bad habit; untruths salving a conscience because they were told for a good cause. My sanity.

John swallowed the progressive gulping fabrication. He retrieved what remained of his dignity, swept up his briefcase in the grand manner of a martyr condemned to earning a living, and no pope could have matched his long-suffering forebearance for us sinners.

A sudden quiet reigned. Benny, Bobby, and Ruff-Ruff kept silent watch as I wiped off trays and doled out cookies left over from yesterday's groaning board. The toaster toasted a poptart for their mother. Who nuked the cooled coffee, and flopped onto a chair restored to an upright position, from where she flaunted dietary rules. The phone rang. The day continued its downhill trend.

"Philippa Saddle here, Victorina."

Mother and mother-in-law had talked it over and decided between them that since the house renovations were going so splendidly and all that, that Thanksgiving should be held at our place (John's and mine) this year. Perfectly honest grounds, I remonstrated the obvious. We had no seating for such a large sit-down meal. Mother Saddle calmly calmed my fears.

"Not to worry. I've been saving this nice surprise for you and John. We (the royal we?) are having delivered to you a diningroom set that has been in the family for simply donkey's years."

The British idiom escaped me, but it did seem to mean that this furniture was ancient. The last thing I wanted in my 'new' diningroom was a hunk of junk. Lying, I had gotten good at, at least since breakfast. Especially if it meant avoiding hurting anyone's feelngs. With the best grace I could muster up I accepted the gift. Thanked her with what I hoped sounded like all my heart. She was so pleased. I was something else that started with a 'p'. No time to scold myself. Benny and Bobby always resented the telephone when it kept their mother's attention away from them. Pure truth when I excused myself to see to them. The Oreos were gone in one way or another. The boys had been prisoners in their highchairs far too long to suit them. A few more conventional pleasantries, a cheery-bye, and my mother-in-law disconnected. Over and out.

Outside. We needed our daily outing. The children needed physical activity. I needed to unwind emotionally. Ruff-Ruff needed bladder relief. Walks were usually a remedy for all of the above. Little did I suspect that that day, inauspiciously begun, was still out to get me. If not right away, certainly in the near future.

Delilah Sealman waved from her front steps, she sat watching a figure in Oshkosh-type, baggy overalls and a billed cap with those earflaps that fold down almost all the way around. Most of the makeshift shingle coverup had been pried away from the porch railing. Some spindles were missng, not a few were damaged. What remained was unique. A row of stylized 'S' shapes were attached, top and bottom, to the porch's upper and lower rail. They resembled nothing so much as squeezed-flat-sideways, wooden geese. Fat stomachs sticking out, all in a row. It was no crime to be neighborly. I pointed at the goose railing.

"I like it!"

Del shouted for us to come and meet Les. All of a jumble, joined together via hands, stroller, and a leash, we staggered up the walk as one clumsy, comic entity. Les paused in his exertions to wipe his forehead with a forearm, and to remove her cap. A brain click. A female? She got introduced as Del's partner in the house venture. Not the expected husband? So what? I chided myself to myself. Women share dorms, apartments, why not the cost of a house? Since it turned out that their furniture was as yet on route, and since Thanksgiving was less than a week off, and since Providence, a.k.a. Philippa Saddle, had provided a last-supper-sized table, why not ask our neighbors to gobble up a turkey dinner with us?

The pair sent a message to each other via the eyes. Del played spokeswoman. Les had a previous commitment. Del had a lot of cleaning to be done before the movers arrived two days hence. I gave her an argument. All the more reason to join us, she being alone and the furniture unpacked. She had to eat, didn't she?

"Are you sure you want me to come? Your whole family will be there."

To my ears this rang as the customary plea to be coaxed a little. I begged, albeit over my shoulder as Ruff-Ruff towed us across bumpy ground towards the nearest tree.

"Please come. We'd love to have you." As I toppled over, "Quick! S-s-say yes!"

My plopped predicament promoted Del's laughter. "Okay!"
How was I to know that I had tumbled from more than grace into what would be another pitfall attributable to that fateful day? Ignorance was bliss. Del's willingness to share in the Thanksgiving meal was a step towards friendship. She had changed a day that had gotten off to a poor start into a day that wasn't so bad after all. Del helped us get disentangled and right side up, much to the children's merriment. We trundled off, finally, to complete our walk in the best of spirits. Nothing on my mind but the walk would be over in an

hour. Leftover macaroni awaited a reheat for lunch. Boys and bottles in their crib beds in double time. Two hours left to be mine alone. That day be darned! No sooner were we home that the brass lion's head rapped against its knocker plate on the front door.

Derek! How could I have forgotten Derek? The temptation to pretend that there was nobody home tested me sorely. For a whole guilt-filled minute. Conscience won. At the door awaited a man who had given up his lunch hour to bring me the wall covering samples. No matter what Derek was, he was a nice—oops! an agreeable fellow. I opened up. Self reproach lingered so strongly as I greeted him that I invited him to join the boys and me for a quick lunch. He was glad to. Better than his acceptance, he kept Benny and Bobby occupied with building leggos while I nuked the macaroni and cheese. Bread and butter, and grapes sliced lengthwise so as not to be child chokers, and voila! we made a fun meal of it. The boys wanted our guest's total attention, which he gave them by talking to them and making faces at them. I think the children sometimes craved company other than mine, as much as I longed for an adult to talk to during the day.

Before Derek left he told me to pick out a lincrusta pattern. He knew a decorator's shop where we could get a good bargain on any item in the binder. If John needed our car, he would be happy to pick me up and drive me to the mall. I opted for the Monday after the Thanksgiving weekend—get that over with first was the idea—and with the condition that we go during Benny and Bobby's nap time. Ma preferred to babysit while the babies slept. Derek flashed his smile.

"Okay. If that works out, it's a date!"

Our trio waved goodbye from the doorstep, reluctantly, as far as the boys were concerned. Ruff-Ruff, collar fingered to keep indoors, wagged a pendulum tail at his new friend's untimely farewell. I failed to see any reason not to be friendly with Derek. Was withholding information the same thing as telling a lie? Maybe, but a hassle avoided meant peace in our time. Mine and John's.

# VI

Anticipatory dread preceded the arrival of the table and chairs gift. The furniture did appear on the day following the 'fate full' day. In retrospect, the beginning of my downward spiral contrary to the old inborn sense of right and wrong this woman lived by. What I had classified as Saddle cast-offs arrived in one full load on one of Uncle Victor's open-bed trucks. I recognized the truck and the driver, Sime. The cargo travelled incognito under plastic wraps, sacking and rope. Legs, leaves, tabletop halves, and twelve chairs in separate swathings and bindings. Adrenaline pumped. Dear Lord, assembly required. John was an academic not a mechanic.

Heavy. Even in its divided-to-conquer state the set was heavy. Just how heavy? Sime's cigarette actually fell out during the off-loading and the inhaling for the haul-in exertion. The hard part done, Sime had the table together and back on its legs in less time than it would take to tell. Complete with its three extension leaves and twelve unveiled chairs all set to protect the table's circumference with shield-shaped backs up and ready. I was impressed. Sime was so impressed that he lit his cigarette and disappeared in a great puff of smoke.

Benny, Bobby, and their faithful canine companion, liked this novel addition to the diningroom. It became an adventure to wriggle between the chairs and to sit under the table. The grapevine carvings on the drop held my attention. I had condemned this superb table sight unseen. Experienced a fleeting comparison vis-a-vis how we sometimes judged strangers unfairly. That realization really was heavy.

Maybe, but at that moment I felt happy and gay thinking of a Thanksgiving dinner served aboard that magnificent table. Oops! Amend that to happier than I had felt for a long time. Why had 'gay' become a dirty word, wondered I. It never used to be. I hummed a snatch from Jeanne Crain's solo from the film 'State Fair'—"But I feel so gay, in a melancholy way-hummmmmmm . . ." 'Fair' brought to mind a picnic. Lunch sandwiches and apple quarters were served, where else? underneath our newly-acquired table. The crumbs had less distance to fall. Ruff-Ruff benefitted from that. I ate topside chewing over the 'gay' besmirching. Cary Grant had said he felt gay in "Bringing up Baby. (Clad in Katherine Hepburn's feathered robe, he had only seemed funny) A book had borne the title "Our Hearts Were Young and Gay". The Victorian's lived in the Gay Nineties. Enola Gay was a brave airplane. Gaie Paree. A gay blade.

Speak of a gay blade, and in popped one. The gay blade in that instance was happy and gay because the furnace at the college had gone on strike and his last two classes had been cancelled. In olden days a gay blade alluded to a dashing swordsman, but was it also a phallic symbol allusion? Here was my gay blade arriving home with a look in his eye that bespoke great expectations. At the exact time when I was perishing for the pause in the day's occupations. Instead of a knitting up of my ravelled sleeve of care, John looked hell-bent on taking off the whole darned sweater, et al. I had just clocked in six solid hours of child and pet care: entertaining, educating, diapering, snacking, aftermath pickups, outdoor exercise and play, letting Ruff-Ruff out and into the backyard on the offchance that he might not be kidding whenever he barked at the back door. Give me a break. I deserved it.

I resorted to tactical verbal manoeuvres rather than an outright denial of John's masculine desires. I did a little sidestep excuse. The car was available. He was home to sit his sons. It was a perfect time for me to run some errands. I needed a restorative breather. Although having sex would get me off my feet, it was not the added activity I needed at that moment. I was in the stimulation overload mode. I needed to be alone. Left alone. I had Greta Garbo's complaint. Before John could get his pro-sex, argumentative ducks in a row, I kissed him soundly and thanked him for giving me this free time. I was out of there.

Where was I going? I had no idea. Once out of sight of house and husband I pulled over to the side of the street around the corner from ours. Hopping onto the freeway held no charms. Shopping was out. The housekeeping allowance was eaten down to its bare bones. I remembered a small strip mall only a few miles away, reachable by side streets. It boasted one of those coffee shops that became so fashionable. The shops offered about a dozen coffees for one's pleasure, as well as donuts, Danish, and muffin noshes. Someone waited on the customers seated on wire-backed chairs at full-moon tables. To be waited on! Yes. That decided it.

I bought a newspaper for its crossword puzzle on the way in. Inside, I made a beeline for the closet of a restroom. Poor planning is running away from home with a full bladder. I had been on a holding pattern until the boys went down for their naps. Doctors warn that child care givers are prone to bladder infections for just that reason. In rebuttal I say, answering nature's call in solitary confinement was a luxury worth waiting for. Another unexpected learning situation among the neo-parental surprises.

The menu had been chalked onto blackboards on the wall
Behind the counter. Choices, choices! Brands with South American names, Hawaiian kona, espresso, cappuccino, au lait, latte, half-caff, and bean blend varieties, spoke in foreign tongues to yours truly.

Whereas, terms synonymous with chocolate—au chocolat, mocha, cacao, malted, these spoke my language. On the verge of settling for the cheapest and most conventional, I stopped short of ordering at someone in the lineup calling my name.

"Vickie! Are you a coffee maniac too, I hope?"

The greeting came from Delilah Sealman. I denied any such virtuosity. I told her I was about to use the tic-tac-toe method. Del chuckled. That bit of infectious laughter began an awareness that Del was fun to be with. In faked conspiratorial tones she urge me to go for the mocha, adding in a villain whisper that it was infused with chocolate, lots of chocolate, and it must be topped with double whipped cream servings. I started a demur. Del overrode it.

"Oh, come on. Les is out of state on that legal case. I feel blue, and you look as if you need something good for your soul, too. It's on me."

When was the last time anyone had divined how down I felt just by looking into my eyes? Del's acuity warmed me through. The coffee we sipped through thick cream dollops kindled a friendship. Both the rich coffee and the spirit with which we shared it were delicious. Delicious to giggle at frothy moustaches frosting our upper lips. Delightful to play oneupmanship on the crazy things that happened while renovating our old houses. Del's house had a switch insid the linen closet that baffled as to what it turned on or off. I had a john that was so old it was impossible to find parts for it, we couldn't afford to replace it yet, so we had to flush it using a pair of pliers. Which my other John kept carrying off. Talk about embarrassing moments! Del claimed that was nothing.

She hadn't seen that the bathtub leaked until she had tried to fill it and the water lapped out from beneath it up to her ankles. Aha! I had a workman whose cigarette acted as a barometer for his emotions. I used a straw between my own lips to show her how. Another sipper gave us a strange look. We were bad. We ordered a second helping. Our senses of humor soared aboard a caffeine high. I had fallen in love with chocolate-laced coffee forever.

Nothing lasts forever. I had to get home. John met me at the front door looking the way he always looked whenever he had been left alone with his two sons for any length of time; relieved, but trying not to show it. The boys had no such inhibitions where showing their feelings was concerned. They hugged me at knee level. Gleeful in greeting.

"Mama! Mamma!" Genoese for 'Mommy'.

I was glad to be reunited, too. The respite from being in their constant company had done me a world of good. They had a surprise for me. We were all going to Madonno's for dinner. No nutrition treason charge valid here. MacDonald's is an okay place to eat, nutritionwise. However, I must admit that so long as I did not have to cook dinner, I would have eaten at any greasy spoon anyone cared to choose, and dubbed the food 'ambrosia'.

Tummies tight with burgers, fries, and shakes, our sons aplashed around in our claw-footed tub. The little rascals thought it fun to spray their parents to soaking wet, too. John helped me dry the slippery wigglers and tuck them into bed. We shed our soggy clothing and skinny-dipped between the sheets to share in a strictly adult romp. Some moments are reminders of how lucky can you get. My John and my boys were my life.

I hadn't intended to keep it a secret, the trip to the mall with Derek; it was just that John fell fast asleep after the fast food. I came down from feeling happily silly. Tell him about my 'date'? Derek had called it a date. Had I made a date with another man? Nah. Derek was gay. Ah, was the operative 'gay' or 'man'? Two sexes made life complicated enough. A third sex? A boggled mind refused to fall asleep. One half of my brain told me that a 'date' with Derek was innocent. That to be in his company should not roil up waves in matrimony's sea. The other half did not agree, expecially in the light of John's strongly expressed antipathy to gays. Good grief Charley Brown! Wasn't the same thing as meeting with an interior decorator? Not a 'date' date, but simply a number on a calendar date. So why was I plotting to borrow Ma's car when she came to babysit and thankful that she would not see a man taking me to the mall? And the fact that I would not have to ask John for our car, so he would not know I was going out, and I could skip the reason of why I needed it. Subterfuge did not become me.

I felt uncomfortable. The bed felt uncomfortable. The whole scheme smacked of Machiavellianism, whereby the ends justifies the means; to wit, I would get the lincrusta I wanted without him upset, and without me suffering the slings and arrows of his self-righteous anger at his wife's direct disobedience of his orders. It was one more bit of deceit I had to try and fit into the puzzle of what was displaying, ever more, an increasingly complex relationship. It wasn't as if, I rationalized, I was going to be sneaking out to meet Derek on a regular basis, or for that matter, to have dealings with any other gay persons.

As far as I knew, and in hindsight it was not far enough, I had no acquaintanceship with any other person who was a homosexual. Oh what a tangled web we weave, when first we practice to deceive—ourselves. A descent into misquotes that welcomed a drowsiness so slow in coming.

# VII

Quote: "Come little leaves," said the wind one day, "Come over the meadow with me and play.

"Put on your dresses of red and gold, "Summer has gone, and the wind blows cold."

A rhyme I rembered from my own kindergarten days. I had turned it into a verse to say and act out, the ad lib action being to pretend to be the wind, then the leaves that ran around the backyard, as fast as toddler legs could go, hugging ourselves and shouting, "Brrrrrrrr!!— The four-legged leaf obliging with counterpoint barks. We ran until we all fell down. Started all over again. Children love repetition. Nursery rhymes are very important in that regard. They teach the correct cadence to the English language when said over and over. Every language is spoken in its own particular rhythm, so nursery rhymes are not the nonsense they seem. Luckily, I discovered the nearest public library before my own nursery rhyme and fairy tale repertoire ran out. It was beyond walking distance, which meant driving John to his college, and picking him up later, but a public library is worth its weight in gold. We could rent books and tapes. It became a weekly trip. We had begun to settle into a routine and to feel at home in our new home.

The leaves clinging to the trees lining our long, onesided street, had obeyed the wind's command to put on their dresses of reds and golds. In costume, they danced and played and fluttered away, leaving their trees behind them. Giant trees. Trees that had celebrated as many, and maybe more falls, than the half-century old houses we fixer-uppers lived in. Joyce Kilmer trees. Trees that shaded. Trees that sheltered. Trees that pleased the senses. That first autumn in our renovated home those trees outdid themselves. They gloriously gift-wrapped themselves in a radiant Joseph-coat splendor.

    Del and Les' house was blessed with a fine maple. It blushed red at the state their house was in, but compensated for its embarrassment by emblazoning the stubbly lawn with a crimson badge of courage. A mere seventeen percent of the earth's surface can boast trees whose leaves turn scarlet. The reds are the first colors to appear, and alas, the first to fall. The elms are fighting a losing battle. The University of Toronto has researched diligently to find a cure for Dutch elm disease. It must be, thought I, some kind of AIDS tree virus that defies scientific solution. I prayed every night that AIDS will be preventable or curable by the time Benny and Bobby are dating. Gold coin imitators on our birch flew away. The gnarled oak in our backyard clung to its brown leaf clusters, refusing to go bare until winter winds did their worst.

    Suddenly, Thanksgiving sat on our doorstep. Our first Thanksgiving in a home of our own, and my first time as chef for a full house. A traditional menu won the draw as the safest bet to include items palate-pleasing to everyone. As a family affair, of course the children had to be included in the preparations. John's contribution began with a lift to the supermarket. He seated Bobby in a shopping cart. I pushed Benny aboard another. John had orders to cruise the aisles to find a favorite or two for his parents' eating pleasure. I had a list. Benny and I eyed the fresh (never frozen) turkeys. The naked and the dead lay in the refrigerated open counter with the dubious attraction of beheaded birds with goosepimple skin. Coward that I was, I let Bobby make the choice. He pointed and ordered me to, "Det duh bid one". I hoisted up all twenty pounds of it. It was a big one. Terrifyingly so.

At the checkout, Benny sat lost amid the big turkey, a few dozen brown-and-serve rolls, pumpkin pie filling in fat cans, Stove Top Stuffing stuffed into large boxes, a net bag keeping twenty pounds of potatoes prisoner, a quart of heavy cream in four cartons, two pounds of butter, two dozen eggs, three broccoli bouquets, four tall candles, ten holiday-motif placements, twenty paper napkins, salt, sugar and flour for the pantr-e-e-e!

John and Bobby, in line behind us, had looted the shelves of the Deluxe Planter mixed nuts, after-dinner mints, potato chips, corn chips, and cheese doodles, cube-packaged cola cans, ice-cream by the blocks, five cookie varieties, jarred hot fudge sauce and a few bananas. John pointed out that he had remembered the cranberries that I had forgotten. I would have been more proud of him if his comment upon scanning the saleslip had been uttered with a plural pronoun.

"Gosh, Vic, you've put a big dent in our food budget for this month."

IT WAS HIS FIRST CRITICISM EVER OF *my* spending. I forgave him, especially since I had a check in my purse from Ma and Pa to help foot the food bill. Reassured him.

"A little splurge is part of the fun!"

Water activities delighted Benny and Bobby. They stood on two chairs at the sink drowning celery, radishes, broccoli florets, et al, destined to become crudiés for the hors-d'eouvres tray. Dried off, they sat in their highchairs wielding butter knives in deeply concentrated attempts to fill the grooves in celery stalks with cream cheese.

My plan was to show them how to make ants-on-a-log by lining black raisins along the cream atop the celery 'logs'. Benny heard the word 'ants', and remembered how horrified his mother had been at an earlier ant invasion into her kitchen. He plucked off an 'ant' raisin and tossed it away in imitation of my shrieks.

"Aahts! Aughhhhh!"

His greatest admirer, Bobby, followed Benny's lead. 'Ant' tossing hilarity got underway in a big way. I couldn't beat them (they were too cute), so I joined them. Most of the dried grape missiles hit the table. Some made it as far as the floor. Why should it come as a surprise that a dog who spurned Super Supper for Pets tongued up black raisins and begged for more? The 'ants' on the table got recycled. I scraped them together, doled them into three piles, and then whisper-hissed,

"Let's be spider monsters and gobble them all up!" Which we did accompanied by snarls and growls. And we all lived happily ever after, or until it was time to go for our naps.

Thanksgiving Eve, John helped by peeling a ton of potatoes. 'Ton' exaggerated, because peeling potatoes was one chore I hated. While John skinned the spuds, his sons and I prepared the next day's dessert. I rolled out the dough, they squeezed, squished, and patted the pastry trimmed-off bits to their hearts' content.

They experimented with nibbly bits of it. A worry-wart mother, I suffered a few qualms at their eating raw dough. I needn't have worried, but when one becomes a mother much needless worry becomes an occupational hazzard. Their digestive tracts survived.

We parents were dead tired by the time I bathed, dried, and put our little rascals to rest, and John had done the same to the turkey. Late as it was, the phone rang. It was Uncle Victor asking permission to bring along two guests to our holiday feast. I asked no questions that might prolong the conversation. Told him his friends were welcome. I, myself, had invited a nonfamily member, a neighbor who would be otherwise alone. The more the merrier? He agreed. I bade him goodnight and hung up.

I got hung up on a head count. Us—four. Ma and Pa—two. The Saddles—three. Uncle Victor and guests—likewise. Del. Thirteen sitting down to one table, one dead by the end of the year. Shades of the Last Supper? I juggled the numbers. Eleven adults at the table. Two children in highchairs did not count as actually sitting at the table. This silly stratagem somewhat allayed my fear that I had received a disaster warning and risked ignoring it.

# VIII

The weather maven for a local t.v. channel had forecast clear roads for the holiday travellers. As so often happens on Thanksgiving day when families are travelling to be together, white stuff floated earthwards. It snowed, except that it was a snowfall so gentle that the feathery flakes held their individual doily patterns and spread a most delicate lace atop the grass, dissolving to mini damp spots if they chanced to touch down on a hard surface. The roads were wet, but they were clear.

The snowfall excited Benny and Bobby. John yielded. He volunteered to take them out into the yard and accepted a duty that was usually mine, the duty of refilling the birdfeeder. Ruff-Ruff did his bit by thwarting the squirrel who regularly stole fat cheek pouches full of our expensive sunflower seed. He sat erect at a distance, his bushy tail a backup prop, his black eyes bright with appreciation for the replenishment grains and kernels trickling into the squirrel-proof, plastic holder. He knew better. He dropped onto all fours, and semaphored his frustration at delay with saucy tail ripples. Such impudence provoked Ruff-Ruff to make a sprint at him, capture eluded by the squirrel's escape artist leap into the safety of our gnarled old oak tree, where he sat listening to Ruff-Ruff bawl him out in barking code.

No less energetic, the boys were perpetual motion pictures. They caught snowflakes on their mittens and on their stuck-out tongues. Good, cheered I through the window. The morning exercise would both tire them out and stimulate their appetites for an earlier snacky lunch, and a slightly advanced nap time in order to accommodate Thanksgiving Day's altered schedule. Dinner was slotted for four p.m. This arrangement allowed for a catch-up view of the football game by the men, a visit chat among the women, and grandparents to lavish affection on Benny and Bobby before we all sat around that wonderful table. Also, Pa, who lately preferred not to drive after dark, could set off for Willoughby Hills while some daylight remained.

My parents arrived early. A manicotti casserole, foilinsulated to retain heat, occupied both Pa's hands and his full attention during its transport from his car to my kitchen. Ma had whipped up little pasta muffs filled with spinach, Romano cheese, mushroom bits, and eggs, held together in a flour-butter-cream paste, submerged in tomato sauce, sprinkled with grated parmesan, and had brought the dish along, "Just in case". There had been a time, not so long ago, when Ma's over-solicitude would have rankled. Having become a mother, I saw her concern from a whole changed perspective. I was her only chick. Besides, the burden in her basket probably was a Génoise, a rich Italian cake, butter-cream frosted, orangey cointreau in palate-pique-ing hints. The hug Ma received surprised her for its enthusiastic embrace. Flustered her to a clarification.

"So who knows for such a big meal with so many people? Better we should have too much food than too little. Who knows what could happen to the cooking, no?"

The potatoes had begun to boil before Uncle Victor came through the front door, his two guests and wine bottles packed in straw with him. Uncle Victor introduced Zelda. The woman had Cher hair unsuccessfully subdued into a french twist, gold loop earrings, a bosom cleavage attractively conspicuous above the top button of a lemon yellow blouse, and her great pair of legs walked upon backless high-heeled sandals. John thought Zelda real cool. A wife can tell. The wine bearer set down his burden. It was Derek, who was Zelda's son. John's cool shot upwards to emulate the potatoes. Ere he could boil over, I herded the newcomers out to the family room to meet Ma and Pa who were supervising their two grandchildren.

Uncle Victor slipped me a check. I handed it on to John. The amount mollified him enough to prevent hyperventilation. He slipped it into the pocket of my old navy dress. For the past three years frayed jeans, baggy sweaters, and makeshift maternity tops had held sway. We really were striving to be independent.

Neither Ma, nor Uncle Victor, paid the slightest attention to our faint denials where money was concerned. Outright refusals would have hurt their feelings. Or so we rationalized. I was saved from a sotto voce dissertation in the kitchen on John's aversion to having homosexuals in his castle by a ringing summons to the phone.

Del was sorry. A pipe had burst in her basement. The yellow pages had finally come up with a Zimmerman's emergency plumbing service (is there any other kind?) listed on-call twentyfour hours a day, seven days a week, extra charges for holidays. No matter what the fee, she had no choice but to wait until Mr. Zimmerman arrived. She iterated her so sorry. I made her promise to come over as soon as she could. She said she would try to make it over for dessert, but please, not to hold up any part of the meal on her account.

Mater, Pater, and Mary Jane entered on a breeze from the open front door, which entrance blew John's on-hold plans to berate me for Derek's inclusion in the Thanksgiving festivities. The thin Mary Jane's black sheath dress optically reduced her to a quasi emaciation. Her dangling handbag twitched about as she sought the loo. Of loos, we had but one, and it was up the stairs I pointed to it. Mary Jane let out a moan, but took the flight. Mr. Saddle, ever gallant, presented me with a cornucopia style fancied fruit basket in order to have a free hand to help his wife off with her cashmere cape. The assortment of fruits had journeyed from exotic lands. No doubt existed that they had been ordered from a classy catalogue. Harry and David's came to mind for some strange reason. One thing to be said for Mrs. Saddle, she always did whatever she did up brown That was her idiom. What doing it up brown meant had to be 'good' for that lady to so do it. She brushed aside my thanks, and passed me, explaining her desire to see her grandsons. My father-in-law hung up the cape on the hall rack and offered to help in any way.

On that bit of friendly encouragement, I handed him the place cards and told him to seat Derek as far away from John as was possible. He chuckled.

"I read you loud and clear, m'lady!"

Derek beside the host might provoke the host. Seated in the nether regions, Derek might not be provocation enough to provoke a scene. We would start casually without Del. No problem to save her a place anywhere at the table. We all sat just as a calmer Mary Jane came down from her trip to the loo. My relief ended mid-sigh. John was announcing his decision to carve the turkey at the table so everyone would get a chance to see the whole bird beautifully roasted to perfection by his wife. He set the platter in front of himself and made a theatrical show of sharpening the carving knife. Did you ever see such a sight in your life, as the nursery rhyme goes, and Ma and I ran after the hot foods in the kitchen to get them started on their passing rounds at the table. The relish tray, cranberry jelly, and other cold offerings, were already on the table. To Ma's on-the-run question as to whether my husband knew how to carve a turkey, I gave her a fervently truthful answer.

"I sincerely hope so!"

Pater Saddle had done jolly good at the placecard seating arrangement. John's place at the table's head was a foregone conclusion. Benny and Bobby on either side of him, ditto. Down the side to John's left sat Ma, to be close to Bobby, then Uncle Victor, Zelda, and Derek. If not completely out of John's sight, almost. The foot was my place. A spot beside me reserved for Del. Along the other side were Pa, Mary Jane, Mrs. Saddle, and Mr. Saddle, who didn't mind being around the corner from Benny. We all joined hands. John prayed a short neutral blessing. Ma and Pa crossed themselves Amen.

John, ever the ham, posed, carving knife and fork crossed above the turkey. He could be a lot of fun when he wanted to.

Ma needn't have worried. With a surgeon's skill he removed the drumsticks and thighs and set them on a side plate. He performed an orchestra leader's virtuoso carving knife and fork wave and waggle, then sliced horizontally off neat breast meat ovals. We all applauded his expertise. He began with Ma. Asked her her which part of the bird she preferred. Ma asked for a little white meat for Bobby, and a little dark meat for herself. Uncle Victor, seated next, laughingly confessed that he was a thigh man. Zelda nudged him with her elbow and said any part suited her. Which choice kept Uncle Victor smiling at her. Taking his cue from Uncle Victor, Derek tried for funny.

"Not the part that goes over the fence last!"

John did not find it funny. Uncle Victor choked on his laughter. Ma Told him to take a drink of his wine. Patted him on the back. John hacked off a thick slab of poultry, thwacked it onto a plate, thrust it at Ma to be passed along. His eyes shot daggers at me. Glinted in accusation. His usually sonorous actor's tones rose to grind out the question,

"And you, Vickie, just what part would you like from all this?"

The host's changed temperament turned all faces towards me.
I didn't know what everyone expected. I told John a small portion would be fine. Pa wanted a drumstick and got it posthaste. Mater Saddle, bless her, took the spotlight off me by asking for a serving from the turkey 'chest'.

Mary Jane took her turn for the worst. She began a tirade on the subject of the annual turkey holocaust . . . jumped up and flew away into the upper regions that housed the bathroom. Her father explained that his daughter was a vegetarian, as for himself, he preferred dark meat and stuffing, and plenty of both, eh wot?

The bowls and platters got passed amid a revived joviality. John periodically dashed to the family room t.v. to report an update on the football scores. The Browns were ahead, another cheering hurrah. Mary Jane zigzagged back into her chair to pick aimlessly at her peas and gravy-less mashed potatoes. The relish dish bearing the celery sticks and black olives came within Bobby's reach. He gleefully eyed its contents. Plucked up an olive and flicked it across the table. Followed by another and another in random toss. Accompanied by,

"Ahhhts! Ahhhts!"

The third flying object hit his paternal grandfather spang between the eyes. Before John's outbreak hit the roof, his father intercepted.

"I say! Ripping good shot, Bobby old man! A cricket bowler in the making if ever I saw one!"

Taking advantage of the moment, Ma unbuckled and snatched up Bobby, explaining during the action that she would take the baby to get his hands washed off. That they were all sticky.

John's mouth opened and a click-click sounded from the brass lion head knocker on the front door. I hurried off-scene to greet Del. She smiled at her warm welcome.

"I hope I'm in time for my just desserts!"

I introduced her to the company, "Everybody, this is Delilah Sealman. She and Leslie are partners in buying the house next door."

Del nodded to everyone in general. "Actually, Les is a little more than that. She's my sig-" stopped her words midsyllable, sensed that the generation at the feast believed the only items that came out of closets were articles of clothing, on the half-beat moment amended her disclosure, "my very best friend."

Drunk or sober? I had begun to suspect that the reason Mary Jane toted her handbag upstairs each time she visited our washroom facility, was not because she needed to redo her makeup. Mary Jane' intelligence operated along the razor's edge. While her mother politely opined,

"A best friend. How very nice for you."

Mary Jane leaned backwards, chin tilted up and forward, nose a-sniff for scandal, eyes at full bat and blink in a major effort to bring Del into focus, lips puckered for emphasis, her voice high-pitched and querulous,

"Do-o-o-o yo-o-ou mean to-o-o say that weeee are l-lesssbians?"

All forking up of pumpkin pie and Génoise cake ceased. Del replied honestly,

"Well, we prefer the term 'gay'.

I had to think Derek meant well, "So do we."
Mary Jane's eyeballs bulged in astonishment, which put a halt to her eyelid activity. A slight wobble to the right and left in her chair gave her the time to organize the words to mouth what her addled brain was thinking.

"Swee Jesus! We are s-s-surrounded by them! I need a drink! S-smdy gemme a drink!"

Derek had to know that he was numbered among the 'them', held no grudge, sprang to his feet offering help.

"I'll get it. What she needs is coffee with lots of sugar."

I figured that what I needed was a hasty retreat to the kitchen, and that the whole kit and kaboodle of us needed coffee. I hurried after Derek.

The party broke up soon after conversation was no longer necessary to ask for sugar an/or cream passes, and the cups emptied. Which happened with embarrassing speed. The Saddles excused themselves on the grounds that Mary Jane had become a little unstrung and should be taken home to rest. Ma told Pa that he had better get on the road before it got any darker. She was looking at John's face when she said that. Zelda instantly accepted Uncle Victor's invitation to go home for a nightcap. I had the feeling that 'nightcap' was cryptographic. Del had disappeared among the general exodus. I wished that I could go home, too, except that I was already home.

Except not home scot-free. The events at that Thanksgiving dinner were etched on my brain for instant replay at any given, or ungiven, moment. From that day forward a weird dichotomy took over my personality. John had blamed me for the 'whole mess'. His formidable rage was out of all proportion. Injustice in any form, to any person, ranked as utterly intolerable within my philosophy on the scheme of humanity and what it was supposed to stand for. I saw John, thereafter, from a slightly skewed viewpoint. He had been unfair. Our relationship underwent a subtle change. The change opened up a chink in my moral armor. Maybe that was the hole in the dike that provided me with the least of plausible excuses to do what I did for Del. If an action goes against one's grain, no excuse is good enough. Unfortunately, I didn't realize that bit of wisdom until long after the fact.

# IX

It was the best of times, it was the worst of times. How many people truly understand that introduction to 'A Tale of Two Cities'? The best of times, and the worst of times, happening at the same time, happened to me. During the half decade following The Turning Point Thanksgiving John was still the man I had wanted to marry. I was the one who was different. Dicken's contradictory declaration exactly described my emotional state. Everything was okay, except that I was not in tune with it. The different drummer syndrome?

Right off, and a-typical for me, I had not the slightest qualm about meeting Derek at the Lake Mall. Ma kept her promise to baby sit and she loaned me Pa's Buick. If I hadn't mentioned the trip to John it was not because I didn't want to rock his boat, it was because the new me thought it was a perfectly okay thing for me to do and I didn't need anyone's permission. Derek hadn't cancelled, so I presumed her would be there.

He was. He even waved to me gaily from where he stood beside his truck in the parking lot. He was holding a space for my vehicle. A November gust, strengthened by the updraft effect of an angle created by a curve in the mall layout, hit

We held onto our open jackets and leaned into it. Once inside, we both fingered our hair-do's back into a neater order. I had no idea of what was typically gay male behavior, so I kept my smile to myself. The motion just struck me as funny. Go figure. Would

John have done the same hair smoothing? I hadn't noticed if he had touched his hair in public. I hadn't a clue. I did know that Derek knew where he was going, and that I had better keep up with him.

We arrived at an arched, triple width entry, sided by chain link curtains which slid across the opening for lockup at night. Metallic gold letters swerved and curved to identify the store as a 'Decorator Paradise'. It held true to its name if one estimated a Paradise as rife with pleasures for one's choice in the wall treatment department. Heavy albums, sample books, swatches held together by ringed spines, wood chips pasted onto cardboard displays, assorted paint chips organized as to colors, racks, gondolas that spun their wares for inspection, this shop had them all. For the customer's added convenience, long tables provided a place to sit. Not knowing where to begin, I sat.

Too much of a muchness did not faze Derek. He headed straight for the lincrusta scroll specimens, his direct approach revealing a familiarity with the store. He lugged armfuls of armsful to where I sat. He unrolled and spread the variously patterned lengths for my inspection. The instructions warned that this material required soaking before being carefully applied to the wall while wet. At least a day should be allowed for it to dry before its finishing with a coat of paint. I expressed my hesitancy over these complex directions. Derek brushed my doubts aside with his offer to put the stuff up for me. No pay. Just for the fun of it. It would only take him a couple of hours, and it was all in the family, wasn't it?

Derek saw that he had drawn a blank on the 'all in the family' reference. He hit his forehead with the heel of his hand.

"Oops! Let the cat out of the bag! Victor has asked my mom to marry him. He plans to give her a ring for Christmas, and they plan to get married in the spring. Hey! We will be step cousins-in-law. See. All in the family."

My memory bank booted up John's vehemence as to homosexuality having no place in our family. Ever. So, here was I, about to get an aunt by marriage who had a gay son. Where did that leave us? An uppermost unease in my mind. I was fine, but what about John when he found out? On the bright side, at least I wasn't out and about on a date with another man. I was merely out buying household supplies with a soon member of the family.

Derek prompted, "Let's decide on a pattern real quick so we can have time to get over to the tearoom. Can do?"

Could do. I opted for the more expensive lincrusta, not because it would play harmony to the pillars' classic lines, but because it was pleasingly different to me. Not your ordinary run of the mill wall covering. The rebel, newly found in me, resurfacing again? What was not to like about an embossed repeat pattern of Romanesque foliage sprayed out between curved lines suggestive of vases around the bouquets. A narrow frieze of metopes and triglyphs underscored each panel. A regularity in contrast to the sweeps and swirls above it. I liked it. It was not too plain, not too fancy, it was ju-u-ust right. I chalked up that phraseology to all the fairy tales Benny and Bobby forced me to read. A wondering intruded. Would 'fairy' tales have to be switched to bedtime stories to be politically correct? Go the way of 'gay' as a synonym for happy?

Thinking of Benny and Bobby reminded me of how fast my

two hours of freedom were flying by. Ma preferred to babysit sleeping children, rather than tear her hair out trying to keep up with boys on the loose. I told Derek I should head for home pretty soon. Derek checked his watch. He put forth the premise that if we placed the order right away we still had fifteen minutes to drop in on his mother's tearoom. He strengthened his logic with,

"She is sort of expecting us."

I gave him no argument. Derek raise his hand and waggled his fingers until he caught the eye of a young man he called 'Tub'. For no explainable reason, the finger waggling put me off. I guess I wanted Derek to seem 'normal' when I was with him. Tub was abnormal in that he was as thin as every woman seems to want to be. His nickname 'Tub' had to stem from some idoscyncrasy other than an allusion to his weight. Tub had dark, lank hair, a bluish shadow hinting at the need for a shave, and wore a folded red silk square knotted beneath a generous Adam's apple. The bobbles performed by this part of his anatomy put me in mind of someone, but who was it? Meanwhile, Derek was instructing Tub to please write up our order according to the wall measurements, assuring the nervous Adam's apple that we would pick up our customer copy on our way out. Added,

"Oh, and give us the company discount. Victorina, here, is a relative."

Derek sidled us between the tables and sample stacks over to the Decorator Paradise's west wall, where a picket gate halted our progress. It swung aside readily to give us entry into a roomy alcove off the main store. Its walls were painted hunter green behind floor-to-domed-celing, white lattice work. Silk ivy leaves, which required a touch to tell them from the real thing, intertwined among these backlit trellises to produce the delightful effect of entering a garden gazebo threaded with sunshine and patterned with shade. The artificial sunlight twinkled from Zelda's earring loops, a-swing as her backless pumps wove her gorgeous legs, et al, between the tearoom's teeny-tiny tables.

One was set with a cosy-clad teapot, finger sandwiches, and pretty pink and white petit fours all in a row. Derek was right at home with these delicacies. In a way, being with Derek was almost the same as being with a friend of my own sex, only better. No underlying sexual innuendo to deal with. Speaking of sexuality, and whatever else that entails, Zelda had it. As the hot tea steamed into pseudo English teacups, an equally hot flash gave me cause to wonder what my Uncle Victor was having to confess to his priest these past few months. Did his penance include having to marry the woman? Nah. I scratched that idea. He could say a hundred Hail Mary's, no sweat, and pay for enough candles for the whole congregation to break out in one. Besides, Zelda exuded the happiness that only glows around a woman who loves and is loved.

The visit lasted the minutes it took to wash down tastes of the miniature goodies, aided and abetted by intermittent sips from the teacups. In short order, I learned three things, not necessarily in order of their importance; Derek's father had abandonned Zelda seven years ago with the apology cop-out that he could not deal with having a homosexual son; that orange pekoe tea is tea made from only the first two tender leaves plucked from the top branches of the tea plant; that Zelda not only loved Derek, she was proud of her handsome son.

Derek and I kept our promise to stop at Tub's station. The cost was bad news. Tub's Adam's apple held steady. My swallower achieved an Olympic-class gulp at the total charge for the lincrusta. The twenty percent discount a notwithstanding drop in the bucket. Plus, the store's policy of a deposit before ordering any materials was punctuated via a shift in the red scarf. I did have Uncle victor's check for a hundred dollars with me—believing that it might pay for the whole thing. I offered to make a quick trip to the bank to cash it to be credited as a down payment. Derek saved me the trouble. He asked Tub if a check from Victor was acceptable if I endorsed it. Tub hadn't needed to say yes. His Adam's apple was only too happy to signal in the affirmative. My signature on the check and on the order form's dotted line completed the transaction. Curiousity killed the cat, but mine sought an answer. On our way out of the mall I dared to ask,

"Who was that red neckerchiefed man?"

"Sime's oldest son. He has six brothers, but Tub is the only one who looks like his dad. Couldn't you tell?"

The weather robbed us of the chance to tell each other any more on the subject of Tub. The wind had added water to its gustiness. Wet splatters pelted our faces and clothing. Derek declared we should make a run for it to the cars. I tucked one arm through his, through wet eyelashes agreed.

"Okay, Cuz! I'm with you!"

A friendship sealed. That sprint loomed large among the best of times on my list.

On the other hand, a worst of times scenario haunted me: the treatment Del had received at the Thanksgiving table. The public organizational activities on behalf of gay rights was comparatively new then. I certainly wasn't aware of the problems peculiar to those living homosexual lives. Lacking personal involvement with any hitch in the scheme of gender irregularities, for a long time the silent majority preferred to keep these enigmas that way. Quiet. Uninformed, I was no different. Even if I had guessed at the state of the union next door, how would I have been able to prepare my family? Even if Mary Jane had kept her trap shut, there still remained John's attitude towards Derek. No matter how I sliced it, I came out to myself as the culprit who owed Del an apology.

I made up a Thanksgiving plate from the leftovers crammed into our refrigerator. Leftovers are for the birds. Some law decrees that must be saved until they go off a bit, or foster visible mold growth, before in all good conscience, they are ripe for the garbage can. Seldom are they used up. On that one occasion I was glad of them. They gave me an excuse to get in touch with Del. Information found a listing for her. No hesitation in answer to my request to pop over.

"Sure. Bring the kids with you!"

Delilah's green-eyed, grey coated cat, meant that Ruff-Ruff stayed in his own backyard, but when the rest of us trooped into the house next door we were made as welcome as the flowers in May. Del plugged in the coffeemaker, allowed the boys the freedom to rifle her pots and pans cupboards, and to chase the uncatchable cat. Outmanoeuvered, the boys sat down to watch a school bus program on PBS. Poptarts occupied them snack-wise. We sat down to coffee and chat. I apologized as if the whole fiasco was my fault.

Del laughed and told me to, "Get over it!" She had gotten over it long ago. It went with the territory. We talked about the injustice The Cracker Basket, a restaurant chain, had committed. Every employee had been interviewed and asked his or her sexual proclivity; gay or straight. Gay, out you went no matter the longevity of time served. A class-action suit had been filed against the company. The company stated that it had fired the gay employees on the advice of a doctor. While Del talked, I wondered if that advice negated the Surgeon General's assurance that AIDS was transmitted sexually or if introduced into the bloodstream, not by eating in restaurants. Scary. Del was saying that Les was part of the suit. Also she was job hunting. Del lived on an income from a trust fund her father had set up for her, knowing she would not have a husband to support her. He had moved to Florida. Communication between them was seldom. Del confided that his worst disappointment lay in the fact that he would have no grandchild. No immortality, so to speak. Del had cast a wistful look at Benny and Bobby. I caught that.

In an attempt to cheer Del's altered mood, I introduced the subject of my one and only teaching job after I had graduated in Education and Nutrition. Major and Minor. Teaching jobs were as scarce as hen's teeth. Nutritionists were on the endangered species list as far as well-paying jobs were went. I was further limited in finding school systems in which to place applications because we wanted to keep our el cheapo apartment, which kept John near the college where he was doing his post-graduate work. A single offer came to fill an opening for an elementary gym teacher. I had accepted it for two reasons. The experience would look good on subsequent resumés, and the curriculum included teaching health. Health correlated with healthy eating habits in my mind. Too late I discovered that the grade five pupils were entitled to Sex Education. My ploy was working. Del's face brightened. She was all ears to hear how I managed such a touchy subject with ten year olds.

I told her I managed to scrape by using the old evasive technique that teachers who don't know what they are talking about use—'classroom discussion'. Del got a kick out of what I learned from the volunteered information. Jennifer and her little brother were forced to watch two Disney tapes every Saturday morning so her mother and father could have sex in their bedroom because her mother worked all week and was too tired at night. Lilith's parents had divorced because her father had sex with his sexetary. One child, whom I called Thelma, until I read her name in the enrollment register, and I suppose she supposed I had a lisp too, held up her hand to ask,

"Mrs. Saddle, what egthacly ith having thex?"

Moira had piped up, "For gosh sakes, Selma, we all know what having sex is! What I want to know is how to look sexy."

I shared with a giggling Del—that was an opening made to order. Eating correctly to have clear skin, bright eyes, pretty hair, a trim body. Right up my alley. I could have stretched the looks bit to cover the whole course. Alas, the teacher's guide book instructed the teacher to use anatomically correct terms for body parts; i.e., genetalia. 'Penis' brought forth wriggles and titters. 'Vagina' put the cap on it. Grace shared her mother's secret.

"When you have a baby it has to come out a small hole in your vagina!"

General assemblage screaming. General opinion—no one was ever going to have a baby. Said with a poor me face for Del's benefit,

"I didn't want to have one, either! But it was too late. I was already pregnant."

Del couldn't decide whether to laugh or not, "But that worked out all right, didn't it?"

I barely got started on how un-wonderful my pregnant condition was: a family started too soon, nausea, a forced resignation from my first job for health reasons . . . ended with the end of the cartoon and Benny and Bobby joining us to see if the adults were doing anything interesting. It was time to go. Del helped get the boys into their coats. Remarked hopefully,

"But it was worth it, wasn't it?"

How had I missed the underlying yearning note in Del's voice? I had rattled glibly on thanking Del for her offer to babysit any time, her offer to borrow her car whenever, and for the coffee break. Hindsight criticized me as self-absorbed and selfish. I was poor material for a best friend. Having Del for a best friend at that time in my life changed that time of my life to one of the best of times.

# X

If someone with Marcel Proust's talent for minutely translating every single emotional nuance involved in the detailed inner workings of a character's train of consciousness connections, in tempo with their transmission from synapse to synapse, if that same someone had shared his expertise with me, more applicable words might have been found to describe explicitly exactly how I was feeling during that critical period of my life. The best this amateur could come up with was an abbreviated confiteor; to wit, a prolonged nervousness perched on Dilemma's sharp horns, from which uncomfortable vantage point I absolutely refused to assume guilt at any level for my actions.

I waited in silence while my hero huffed-and-he-puffed his suit-jacket sleeves down into the flannel-lined arms of his toggle coat. While people were starting to become versatile in computer-speak, I was becoming well-versed in nursery speak. The huffing and puffing over, John's hands visibly awaiting the handing over of his briefcase, I hesitantly dared a halftruth.

"The wallpaper will be up when you come home tonight. I-I thought it would be nice (mater-speak) to get the parlor done before Christmas." This sounded 'good' to John.

Derek was due to arrive. A feeling of 'a lot he cared how I might have to struggle with hanging the lincrusta' mingled with relief that John had departed before Derek showed up.

Derek came complete with all the paraphernalia necessary to do the job. He was neat to a fault. His prissiness in the preparations rather strained my patience, but free labor was free labor. He canvas covered the oak floor, removed the bookcases after emptying them too carefully deliberate, and unfolded a portable table, wiped off every inch of its work surface. The children did better than I did. They were content to watch the preparations until Derek filled a wide, shallow pan with water to dampen the lincrusta. Water acts as a magnet to toddlers. I pulled the playpen into the area between the diningroom and the parlor, giving Benny and Bobby a front-row advantage to watch Derek's performance. I seized the opportunity to clear the breakfast dishes. A discouraging word followed quickly. Derek had Benny by the hand. He apologized.

"I'm sorry. I didn't notice Benny climbing out. He's okay. Just a bit wet."

A bit wet was putting it mildly. That was the first time Benny had succeeded in climbing out of the playpen. I hoped it didn't mean that escape from his crib was soon to be a fait accompli. Benny's main stress stemmed from his writhing attempts of get out of Derek's grip. That splendid pan of water awaited. Bobby, alone in the hated playpen, set up a splendid howl. I surrendered all thoughts of a cleaned kitchen.

"Give me five minutes to get Benny into dry clothes and we are out of your hair out of here."

Bundled to the eyeballs—another hated confinement, stuffed into the double stroller—an additional resentment, leash hooked to the handle—Ruff-Ruff's pet peeve, we set off with a brisk tail wind scooting us forward. I figured if Derek worked at his own measured pace, we would need to sally forth for about thirty minutes, amuse ourselves in the schoolyard for thirty more, and return at about the going-out rate, we all could eat any early lunch, naps could follow, and the wallpaper hanging could proceed unhampered into the early afternoon. That plan would allow Derek to be gone before John came home.

Outward bound, we saw one eye peering at us from behind a lace curtain. It stopped us in our tracks to wave at it. An elderly hand waved back. No other sign of life on the street. Dead brown leaves, motivated to topsy-turvy forays against our wheels and feet by a williqaw wind, scritched and scratched at the silence. Two squirrels played mad-dash tag in the school yard. It hit me that surely this couldn't be the mating season?

The playthings at the school yard had been dismantled. Only the geodesic climber had been left to tough out winter. Released, Benny and Bobby staggered over to it. Their bulky snowsuits slowed them to men-walking-on-the-moon motions. The strengthening wind toppled them over. Padded, as they were, no one got hurt. Getting back onto their feet was a laughing matter the first few times. They soon tired of that and turned cranky.

A nasty headwind buffetted us for the trek homewards. Ruff-Ruff's ears blew horizontally straight back. Sudden squalls swirled our breath away. I adjusted the boys' scarves over their mouths and noses. I leaned my weight into the push of the stroller before I discovered it was easier to protect the children by turning the handle to face the wind and towing the stroller with my back to the wind. The elements showed no pity. A cottonball snowfall hitchhiked on the gale. It blurred visibility to practically zero.

Even so, I saw Derek coming toward us. His appearance lowered my high anxiety. Just how high it had been hadn't registered until I realized how grateful the sight of a rescuer coming to meet us hit home.

Winter had arrived full force. The snowstorm dressed our whole world in white, and us to match. We wore whitened coats and hats, beneath them—powdered hair and eyelashes. The white stuff tracked inside on our boots. Good old Ruff-Ruff licked up the slush before our front hall needed a mop up. He seemed to find the cold drink tasty.

Benny and Bobby savored the leftover meatloaf, reheated peas, bread spread with real butter, and apples quartered and cored. The smug nutritionist in me informed Derek it was because children liked food that was easy to chew. Derek replied with sonething like, 'no kidding?', then the opinionated decorator in him told me that he would be back in two days to paint the lincrusta. No by your leave. I put it down as tit-for-tat. Nobody is perfect.

Derek did perk what I judged to be pretty good coffee while I settled the boys, with their John-forbidden bottles-into their cribs. Derek invaded my territory.

"Do you always buy your coffee in three-pound cans?"

Of course I did. The nerve of him. He had to know every thrifty housewife buys large economy sizes to save on household expenses. I condescended to explain this fact to him. He took no offense. He expostulated on how coffee should be bought in small, sealed amounts, and kept in the refrigerator of freezer for the best results. Coffee quickly deteriorated to stale and bitter if not stored properly. He tactfully did not equate the state of my coffeemaker to his next remarks, but I got his nit-picking message. He revealed that coffee contained oils. Stepped on my professional toes. As if I didn't know that! He didn't notice. Went on about how oils adhered to pots and filters, which can ruin the mellowness of even the most expensive coffees. I almost got on my high horse. Dismounted because the caffeine in his very good coffee had kicked in. Congeniality revived.

I readily acquiesced to his idea that I try a few sample packets of coffee his mother used in the tearoom. Agreed with his suggestion that we both paint the lincrusta two days hence, while the boys napped, so that the job would by done before John got home. No dummy, he. I would demonstrate that I was not slow on the uptake, either. I promised to scrub the coffee making equipment to crystal cleanliness. Told myself that I would have done it for Christmas without him telling me my duty. My emotions had just run the gamut from gratitude, to animosity, to friendly reconciliation, and back again. In between coursed telepathetic gaps that only a writer with the delicate precision of Marcel Proust could have filled in.

## XI

Christmas is Christmas. Christmas isn't what it was, and Christmas wasn't what it is. What Christmas is, is too close to Thanksgiving. Why hasn't some senior senator seen that and seen about setting Thanksgiving at an earlier date, seeing that people are seeing about travelling exactly when November sees fit to turn the scenery to winter. These thoughts should be considered as retrospective and attributed to a brief encounter with Gertrude Stein's thought processes.

    The idea that Del's car was at my disposal was to blame for that exposure. The use of a car made it possible to take a weekly trip to the public library without the taking Daddy to work and fetching him at work day's end. We three going, we three coming, and we-we-we round tripping it all the way home. Disney video tapes ran neck and neck as favorites with loaner picture books. The tapes could be kept for a week. This time frame fit my idea of not taking too much advantage of a good thing. My bonus was spare time to do household chores while the t.v. babysat, and the free use of old classic movies provided me with an evening's entertainment that also spared us budget stress, and this allowed John to work on his papers guilt-free. An ideal arrangement.

    "Waiting For The Moon", a borrowed tape, portrayed a living arrangement of another sort, the relationship between Gertrude Stein and Alice B. Toklas, during the time they lived in the French countryside. As it happens in any household, an estrangement occurred via an ill-timed remark and hurt feelings. What happened next between the two women filled me with envy. Miss Stein said to Alice B. that she wanted to ask her to do something for her. Alice B. immediately replied, "Yes."

Gertrude Stein responded with words to the effect that she hadn't yet asked the favor.

Alice B. informed her that it didn't matter. The answer would always be yes.

How often did that sort of selflessness exist between two people? Wondering at it, I found it wondrous, indeed. Neither John nor I ever had said 'yes' to each other's proposed projects right away. Mostly, we argued why they wouldn't work, or why one of us didn't want to do whatever the other wanted to do. Costs, time, unsuitability. I wondered why we couldn't have totally trusting relationship. I truly wanted our relationship to be unconditional and loving. I would discuss it with John. See, even thinking thusly, I had blown it. I determined to set this new attitude by setting the example. The very next person who asked me to do him or her a favor, I would say yes without further ado.

Much ado about something, and much ado about nothing. Such constituted the dichotomy that made a house divided during the prechristmas weeks of that particularly remembered yuletide. Christmas held precedence as to the important 'somethings' in so far as I was concerned. As far as John was concerned, nothing superseded "Much Ado About Nothing", the no-royalty-to-pay play chosen as the season's drama for performance at the community college where he taught. Students as actors attracted relatives as a paying audience which contributed funds to the not-for-profit institution. Rehearsals lay claim to John's every waking moment. Maybe invaded his dreams. He talked in a foreign language as he slept. Words like forsooth, anon, whither, and varlet.

As his goode wyfe, I reasoned rightly so. It was his job. His job was our bread and butter. As a good sport, I tried to accept my lot in the spirit of Christmas, albeit a spirit somewhat familiar as Dicken's lamenting ghost of Christmas Past. Into my daily routine's full schedule, I programmed card mailing, present shopping, and the tree trimming overload. At least it was not my turn to whomp up the festive board. I had more than done my bit towards family togetherness at the now imfamous Thanksgiving. Was it my fault if a few members had become a tad unglued? That problem was their problem. I had no problem with what was their problem. The bottom line still was that any quandary connected to the Christmas dinner that year belonged in Mater-in-law's lap.

As usual, whenever Mrs. Saddle was faced with a social obligation requiring expended energy, that smart lady let her money do the walking. What her affairs lacked in the personal touch, they more than made up for in sophisticated elegance. Moreover, Fate was ever kind to her. For starters, Uncle victor circumvented the necessity for her to invite Derek, a guest who had upset her son at the Thanksgiving table, by announcing his intention to join his intended at her sister's home, for the dual celebration of his and Zelda's engagement and Christmas Day. Mary Jane, my offbeat sister-in-law, was attending AA meetings. A sober Mary Jane should pose no threat to dining etiquette. Del would not be alone. Les was coming home for Christmas, and the pair had their own plans. I thought Del revealed the plans part in case I was thinking of ways to include her in the family dinner one more time. For further proof of Mrs. Saddle's inordinate good luck, she had succeeded in getting reservations for Christmas dinner at the ultra snooty exclusiveness of The Old Mill Road Century Inn.

Lucky for her. Unlucky for me. Nothing was coming out of my closet posh enough to wear amid members of upper-class society.

Thanks to Vance Packard, we all know a pecking order is alive and thriving in America. The faithful old wool dress had met its Waterloo at Thanksgiving. It did not react satisfactorily to grease spot removers, and the nervous perspiration rings in its armpits were permanently indelible. When I mentioned my despair at dress hunting and trying on, I did not mention that the large part of the despair was hunting and trying on with two toddlers in tow. Del did the weirdest thing. She looked me straight in the eye and said, "Yes."

Honestly, it had not crossed my mind to ask her to babysit. For one reason, the use of her car was a great favor. For reason number two, John had forbidden me to have Del in our house. That was the reason the kaffeeklatches took place in her house. Her 'yes' left me open-mouthed but silent. Del's eyes had sparkled . . .

"C'mon. You know you want me to watch the children. I'd love to. It'll be fun. You can take as long as you like."

Who would refuse such an offer? I didn't answer. I was trying for a way to explain John and the house taboo. Del knew that.

"It will be easier for me if they stay here. You know, getting lunch and all. Just bring some diapers and their blankies and I can put them down for a rest on the couch in front of the television set."

And so it came to pass that I received what was for me the greatest gift anyone could give me at that stage of child raising, the gift of free time to do all the things I had to do to make ready a Christmas for my family. What possible gift could I give in return to qualify as a sharer in 'The Gift of the Magi', soulmate generosity? I vowed to myself that if I ever found out what gift it was I would say, "Yes!" No questions asked.

The quest for life is fraught with questions. Much questioned are the reasons for being. Unanswered questions. Questionable answers. Gertrude Stein may not have questioned this state of affairs, but I did. I believed at that time that too many questions were just too darned many questions to handle. And the really big question—was I right, or was I wrong to do what I did—was a question still ahead into my future. Oh, how I was to wish that I would get one wish simply by saying,

"Now, out damned question!"

# XII

I had to ask myself whether or not John would ever leave. A victim to the boomerang syndrome, he made several false starts before he finally drove off to work. He returned once to retrieve his play notes that he had forgotten to put in his briefcase. In a second entry he dashed back through the front door to pocket his wallet on the upstairs bedroom bureau. Thrice, his curtain call, to remind me that rehearsals would run late. Three times an exit, three cheek kisses for me, and three times worked the charm. He was out. I was so ready to leave for the mall that I could hardly wait to see the last of him for a few hours. Blankies, bottles, beddy-bye teddy bears, and two cartoon videos stuck out above a packed bag. Diapers and wipes went without saying.

The boys put up no argument at being left with whom they had renamed DeeDee. They waddled right off to scare up the cat. If they noticed that Mama was leaving but would be back soon they gave not the slightest apprehensive hint at their abandonment. A bit of a downer, that. It caused me to hang around telling the sitter that Ruff-Ruff had been out, telling her what exactly was in the bag, telling her what time the boys—Del cut me off at the pass. She told me to get going. I did. I climbed behind the wheel of her Mustang wallowing in self pity at the ingrate feeling aroused by my sons and Del who seemed as glad to be rid of me as I had been happy to see the back of John. I suffered from that old Jimmy Durante feeling. Did you ever get the feeling that you wanted to go, and then you got the feeling that you wanted to stay? It seemed a wasted effort to make a try at retrieving the eager anticipation I had felt in expectation of freedom for a day.

I needn't have worried. The mall decorations performed their magic act. Abracadabra! Reality blinked into a twinkling fairyland. Trees aglitter to be eyed, spiced aromas to please the nose, lilting carols were music to my ears, touching displays. Pleasures to pleasure all five senses. It was an enchantment spread out among the throng, multiplied a hundredfold to bewitch Amy Tan's one hundred secret senses. The whole schmear was artificial, designed specifically to loosen purse strings. I knew that, but I fell under its spell. I set off with renewed fervor to find a dress that would not put me to shame at the Old Mill Road Inn.

The dresses dangling from hangers on circular and linear ranks in this season to be jolly, seriously competed in the bridesmaid category to win the 'wear it once, hang it in closet forever' purchase. I explored, fingered, and tried on enough weightily beaded, heavily sequinned, tinsel spangled, gold braid trimmed, tasseled silver, jewel button dotted, slinky satins, downy velvets, metallic lamés, handkerchief hemlines and flaming silks to sink the proverbial ship. Besides being fabricated of materials too chic to wear to the library or to McDonald's, the styles ran to short enough to bare one's ass-k me no questions, to cuts that left expanses of pneumonia-inviting skin in the back, or left nothing to the imagination in the boob area.

The mob thickened as the minutes ticking towards noon thinned. It was literally shoulder swimming upstream to thread a passageway to the last-hope department store at the same end of the mall as Decorator Paradise and Zelda's tearoom. Derek had the ability to ace the "Where's Waldo" picture puzzles, for he picked me out of a crowd scene that would have thrilled Breughel's artistic heart. In a human pinball play he bump-bump-bumped his way through the human obstacle course, waving and calling, "Vickie!" The wreck of the hesperus didn't begin to challenge the damage done to the hairdo from pulling dresses over my head. My face had to have mirrored the hopelessness reflected back at me as dress after dress met rejection. We reached each other. Derek smiled his Crest smile at me. Made me smile with his imitation of my in-laws.

"Wot you need, Luv, is a nice hot cuppa tea!"

Christmas countdown precluded ongoing construction or removation as uppermost in people's minds. Derek, umemployed temporarily, was helping his mother, Zelda, to cope with the overflow tea and lunch bunch packing her tearoom. Standees clustered in a line at the white picket gate waiting their turns to sit and sip. It paid to know the owner's son. He took me right through to the tiny kitchen, lifted me off my feet and onto a high stool at the work counter. Resuming his role as a waiter wearing a crisp white shirt tucked into charcoal chinos, Derek deftly set a steaming Earl Grey and a red and green vegetable quiche slice before me. He gave me no chance to cry on his shoulder. He ordered me to tell him my problem in ten words or less.

"Need a dress. All too fancy. Looked everywhere."

I ate. He sped from table to kitchen to table. Zelda planted a pecky kiss on my cheek in passing. Put a helping of plum pudding and hard sauce with temptation's reach during a second pass. I savored it slowly. Drank a second cup of tea. The diners dwindled. Derek removed his leather apron, told his mother we needed twenty minutes to find a Christmas Day outfit for me. What sort of fool was this? crossed my mind. It would take a genius to find appropriate apparel in the right price range in twenty minutes. The genius commanded,

"Walk this way!"

Easy for him to say. I lacked his stride and broad shoulders. He took my hand and towed me along in his wake to a store beneath a sign, 'TOPS & BOTTOMS". A so-called last-minute Christmas sale was in progress, although Christmas was still twelve days away. The main attraction? Tables and shelves stacked to one's eyeballs with sweaters knit in Christmas colors and patterns. Their sixty-nine to ninety-eight dollar tags bore red-line slashes to prices that were one-third off.

The price was right. Derek informed me to look at sweaters, I didn't need a bottom. He answered my question mark eyebrows by reminding me that my mid-calf, denim skirt he had seen me wear, would do fine. His slightly off-putting authoritative side came into play again. He didn't need to tell me facts I already knew. True, I had forgotten about the skirt, but I knew that denim blue would go well with these sweaters' colors. He continued right on about how a sweater would be comfortable, yet dressy. I didn't like it when he nixed the few hip-length pullovers I held up, I guessed he thought for his approval. I held my tongue because he was trying to be helpful. At first, his selection for me went down the wrong pipe, but when he somehow managed to clear a space for a look at myself in a mirror, I saw that he was right in his assumption that the medium weight knit in a vivid blue yarn, sprinkled with snowflakes and accented with red holly berries, was a flattering garb that fit the occasion. Wide-ribbed mock turtle neck, ditto at the cuffs and the waistband, did show off my waistline that I had struggled to return to an almost prepregnancy measurement. In his opinion, the shorter sweater endowed me with a nice long-legged look beneath the A-line skirt's longer length. This struck as a too personal comment, but he was right. This sweater absolutely was the best find. I tried not to make my thanks sound too grudging. I bought his advice and the sweater wholeheartedly. Charged the forty-six dollars plus tax. The whole transaction had take only twenty-one minutes. Derek smiled me an 'I-told-you-so smile. He knew he was clever, but I gave him vocal credit on that account. It seemed the least I could do to smooth over the mixed emotional bag he sometimes caused me to carry. John would have dismissed the whole shopping thing with a do whatever I thought best. Was I comparing apples and oranges? I simply didn't know. Both men were smart in different ways.

It didn't take a genius intellect to know I had stayed too long at the fair. If the boys had slept at all on Del's couch, they would most certainly be awake this late in the afternoon. Probably cranky and missing their mother. Working stiffs were in full migration from Cleveland towards the suburbs. A horrendous, bumper-to-bumper traffic unstrung anxiety for any driver nuts enough to think she could make a fast run for her destination.

My deodorant had run out of power by the time Del's trusty Mustang ran onto the short driveway of the house next door to mine. Del welcomed me at the front door. I stepped inside expecting the worst. The worst turned out to be that Benny and Bobby weren't ready to go home. They had been playing a game of rolling a big ball to each other while sitting, legs spread, on the floor. They want DeeDee to sit back down and play some more. Benny sullenly submitted to DeeDee putting on his jacket. Bobby actually cried and struggled against being zipped up. He didn't stop until Del hugged him and promised that he and Benny could come visit again real soon. Checked it out.

"They can, can't they?"

They could, but I steered them homewards with another attack of mixed emotions. The little traitors. But they were my traitors, and Ruff-Ruff, at least, was hysterically glad to see me. So what if it was desperation to go out to relieve himself, and the sight of me spelled relief?

The boys had added DeeDee to their vocabulary, and it was a break for me that John did not hear them saying their now favorite person's name. Both Benny and Bobby were asleep in their cribs before John arrived home from the late rehearsals. If he failed to ask how our day had gone, it was one more reason to thank my lucky stars. I took my cue from the fatigue lines etched on his face, and decided to refrain from asking him the same question. He told me, anyway.

Up to this point, the play rehearsals of "Much Ado About Nothing" had been dialogue-reading practice sessions. On that day, the day that had so embittered the director lying in bed beside me, the cast performed a run through of adding action to the speeches. The redheaded, freckled-face kid, who was made to order to play Benedict, had evinced a major drawback. He could not gallop. John was using the old Monty Python method, whereby knights on horseback galloped with their own legs. Geoff, as Señor Benedict, couldn't gallop worth a hey diddle diddle. My translation of his ineptitude. It did not amuse John. In an effort to be helpful, I commented from a store of child development skills read in Education one-o-something. He listened as I told him how physical skills developed in sequential order. Sometimes, a step got bypassed; such as, galloping. If a child could skip, chances were that he was ready to learn to read. John wanted to know,

"Could you teach this guy to gallop?"

I was far too busy to try to teach a guy to gallop. The tree wasn't bought, much less trimmed. Presents from Santa waited impatiently in their hidey holes fro wrapping paper and ribbons and bows. Uh-uh! No way was I going to waste time dragging two children over to the college and back to watch some Shakespearean varlet galumphing hither and thither and whither. I stalled for time.

"I have a better idea."

"What? I can't tell Geoff he doesn't have the part."

I reminded my beloved that yea, verily, and forsooth, the sarcastic and mysogynistic Benedict did not ride overly much in the play. Why couldn't the man gallop in any old whichaway, blaming his horse in a way that played up Benedict's biting wit? The play was a comedy, wasn't it? Reticent allowance on John's part that it might work. He hadn't known I had been shopping with Derek, but Derek must have lurked in his subconcious, maybe the result of seeing all those men in tights, whatever the reason, John could not resist a sarcastic goodnight comment.

"I'll bet that guy, Derek, can prance like anything."

I didn't know about that. One thing for sure he was savvy when it came to clothes. I mean, how many men knew from A-line skirts? I kept silent. The last thing I wanted John to know was that Derek had selected the outfit I was going to wear to his mother's Christmas dinner Party at the Old Mill Road Century Inn. It was just possible that he might leave me forever. I snuggled up to John's back. Snuggling up to John was one of our marriage's greatest comforters.

# XIII

T'was the night before Christmas. Finally. T'was especially memorable in that it was the first Christmas Eve excitement evident in our two sons. No rehearsals for John meant us as a family group to trim the real, live, Christmas tree. Benny was ecstatic at being encouraged to hurl tinsel, hit-or-miss recklessly, at the tree branches. Bobby bumbled about picking up dropped silver strings, making a commendable try at emulating his hero big brother. Their father's frame of mind had improved due to Sir Benedict's deft acceptance as to how to ride his wayward steed. A clown at heart, he knew exactly how to put the fault for the clumsiness on his 'horse'. The whole cast had laughed fit to bust, a sure prediction that the audience would find the bit funny, too. The gambit also provided an opening for the actress playing Leonardo's niece, who was Sir Benedict's antagonist and stern critic, to flaunt the knight's doltish capers with an equally comic body language of her own.

We applauded John when he ordered in Pizza. Awaiting the cheese and pepperoni advent, we transferred the two highchairs from the kitchen to the diningroom table. Benny and Bobby toted in styrofoam plates and cans of Coke. Pizza has been declared an acceptably healthy meal by the food experts. The Coke was okay because it was Christmas Eve and we were celebrating. The pizza arrived. I dealt out the meat-dotted triangles. John Poured cola into the boys' lidded cups with the little spouts for nonspill drinking. One small step towards graduation from the bottle. John plugged in the colored lights strung about the tree. Lit a second string outlining the arch between the diningroom and the tiny parlor. Brought to rainbow life the bulbs encircling the Corinthian pillars. I switched off the overhead fixture. From where we sat eating pizza we enjoyed a splendid view of our lit tree in front of the parlor's front window, the scene framed in crayon-box colors along the archway and up the pillars. The boys stared in silent-night wonder under the spell cast by this kaleidoscopic display. Recovered sufficiently to munch happily to see such fun. Well, the dish didn't run away with the spoon, but the crumbs that took flight to the floor contributed to Ruff-Ruff's eating pleasure. T'was, truly, one of the best nights before Christmas ever.

Except for one minor snag. Funny in recall. Maddening at the time. With the children all snug in their beds, John settled down to piece together the two plastic ride-on toys, propelled by walking the feet and non-threatening to whatever door jamb or furniture leg that got in the driver's way. As for truth in advertising printed on the boxes, 'some assembly required', forget it. In all honesty, the instructions should have read, 'hours of mind-boggling direction translation required'. No adept, John, at things mechanical, but he began patiently to unbox and decipher.

During his keeping-his-cool period, I brought forth my presents cache which I had kept hidden in Del's linen closet. Little pitchers had big ears, and even bigger eyes. Children are experts at finding forbidden items. My own eyes beheld a gift-wrapped box that I had not stashed in with my lot. The tag designated it: To Vickie from a secret admirer. Del, and her sense of humor, of course. I snapped off the give-away tag contemporaneous with the snap of John's patience. Rescue required.

The ride-on instructions were written in three languages besides English. They might as well have been in hieroglyphics. It took two intelligent adults with two degrees to prove it, two hours to put together those two ride-on toys. We did beat Cinderella's time by one minute. As we were turning around to toast each other with Uncle Victor's Thanksgiving wine leftovers, the clock struck midnight.

"Merry Christmas to all", said we, "And to all a goodnight!"

Goodnight, indeed! While both Ma and Pa settled in for a long winter's nap, Ma was the only one wearing a cap. A thinking cap. The idea of my oversight kept me awake in the dark. Why hadn't I remembered to buy even a token gift for Delilah Sealman? What was the matter? If nothing out on the lawn went a-clatter, my conscience certainly did. I lay chiding my idiotic self for being so forgetful as to overlook a gift for someone who had turned into a very good friend. It was my own fault that sleep shunned me, and it served me right. I believed it was insensitive clods like me who had inspired Dickens to coin the phrase, 'Bah! Humbug!' My Christmas would not be merry until I had found a way to make it up to Del for this omission. 'Twas the least I could do.

## XIV

Came the dawn. Where is it written that children own the responsibility to be up at the crack of it on Christmas morning? That lacking reading skills and the ability to tell time, they still know that tradition demands obedience to this rule? Benny surprised his parents by arriving at our bedside to wake us up. His climbing out of the playpen had advanced to conquering his Mt. Everest crib sides. This was one step in childhood development I had hoped would be delayed.

Despite John's, "It's too early. Go back to bed." the children brooked no delay. Bobby, hands atop his crib rail, jumped up and down like a cricket on a string in thwarted efforts to clear what kept him prisoner while his big brother was free. Nothing for it but to surrender and get up. Robe and slipper clad we trooped downstairs. John turned on the Christmas lights. I turned on the coffee maker. The bright yellow plastic rideons turned the boys on. They had to be coaxed to tear the paper off their other presents. Once the savage fun of tearing the wrappings was over, the package contents lacked the allure of the ride-ons. They had been worth the assembly trouble.

Benny could make his go. Bobby couldn't. No problem. Bobby had discovered a latent talent. With his tiny fingers and much perseverence, he could unscrew any screw—screws holding knobs to cupboards, screws attaching accessories to the vacuum cleaner, screws in the toilet tank handle, even the screws fastening legs onto furniture. While Benny rode a circuitous route from the parlor, down the hall, through the kitchen where his parents tried to wake up with coffee, and full circle back to the parlor, Bobby was having a different kind of go at his frustrating ride-on. Imagine our surprise to find that after our superhuman efforts to put the toy together, Bobby had taken it apart in about twenty minutes. We were back to square one. I hurried off to retrieve the assembly instructions from the trash. Hurried the children to a late breakfast/ early lunch. Made haste to move naptime forward, the dawn uprising helped camouflage the earlier hour, but it was all in aid of arriving on time at The Old Mill Road Century Inn. My strategy failed, somewhat, because Benny kept climbing out of his crib. John took over. His idea worked. He lowered the crib side lest Benny fall in his escape attempts, and parked the rideon beside the cot so that Benny could see it would be right there when John told him he could get up. I waited. No Benny appeared. John showered. I peeked into the boys' room. Benny was asleep on the floor beside his indoor transportation.

The opportune moment had arrived to open the present from Del. When John had signified his intention to take a quick shower, he really meant a quick shower. He caught me unfolding the tissue paper cradling a soft cashmere scarf. Towel corner working on one ear, he commented,

"Nice. Who gave you that?"

His slippered feet had given me no warning of his approach. I uttered the first answer that popped into my head.

"Ma."

John's wet hair rubbing went on hold long enough for his remark, "I thought your ma and pa gave us money?"

"They did. But I think Ma wanted to give me something, you know, kind of personal."

"Oh. Well, get dressed, kiddo, my mother has the dinner reservations for two o'clock."

My lying had slid into an easy habit. Sadly, it had evolved into including other people as accessories after the fact.

"Please don't mention the scarf in front of Pa. Maybe
Ma doesn't want him to know that she is buying extra gifts."

John bought that. "Okay. But let's not be late, vick."

That episode left a loose end leading to asking Ma not to tell John that her daughter had bought an expensive scarf for herself against her husband's budgetary orders. Whoever said, 'Oh what a tangled web we weave, when first we practise to deceive', hit it right on. And this deception was a drop-in-the-bucket, minor deception when compared to my deception to end all deceptions. Every goal, albeit wrapped in future's mist, is achieved by blindly advancing towards it in small steps, one at a time.

At that moment, large, fast steps were the order of that Christmas Day. No fooling around, despite a husband's naked body showing inclinations to do so. Evasive action taken in getting right to make-up application and to cover up temptation with my Christmas sweater. A pinned up hairdo contributed a more formal fit befitting the occasion. Waking Benny and Bobby before they had had their sleep out was not a no sweat situation. I thought, deodorant, do your stuff! It was a fight to the finish to get the two resentful strugglers into their new clothes, exhausting to get them into the car—leaving their ride-ons behind them, and a major battle to click their seat belts together to restrain them in their carseats. John scolded. They cried. I produced two nippled bottles filled with Hi C. John disapproved.

"Isn't that rewarding negative behavior?"

A tired voice agreed. "Yes. It's sort of like having sex Saturday night with a husband who has been uncooperative and grumpy all day."

Silence kept a tremulous truce. The non-speaking peace held on all the twenty-mile drive to the Old Mill Road. The boys had nodded off after sucking down their orange drink. My bone weariness had put a damper on making an effort to talk. John, probably in review of the rewarding negative behavior as it applied to our sex life, had figured out that his best strategy lay in proving that he was neither uncooperative nor grumpy, and wisely kept his mouth shut.

The Old Mill Road Century Inn is open all year round. It presides over about three acres in the middle of nowhere. I use the present tense because I think that the inn is still in operation. It stood fifty feet or so back from Old Mill Road. A blacktopped, semicircular driveway allowed car passengers to be dropped off at the front door. A spur branched off to a parking lot to the west side of the building. Fieldstone blocks set the inn's walls solidly square. Quoins dressed its corners. A rusticated doorcase, in optical illusion, heightened and broadened the oaken entryway. A pennyfarthing window set in the door's planking eyed all comers through leaded panes. A concrete balustrade fronted what once must have been a formidable house. Up the five shallow steps we climbed, as Alfred Noyes' Highwayman, "Up to the old inn door".

The house had defied time for more than a hundred years. The mill, if one had existed, hence the name Old Mill road, had not fared as well. Nary a foundation trace nor millstone fragments have been found to this day. However, a river flows in a steady current at the bottom of the inn's English garden. It wends its way more or less parallel to the Old Mill Road. Where waterpower abounds, so may it turn the wheel that moves the stone that grinds the grist behind the house that some miller Jack built. A proserous Jack. A man with an eye for a touch of whimsy? For the details on the stone inn fit no classic architectural style.

We four surrendered our outerwear to a cubicled coatcheck person. We advanced on the maitre d' sentinel behind his chest-high pulpit. I adjusted the waistline ribbing of my Derek-selected sweater, thought to my self how Derek would have nailed the inn's exterior as baroque or Georgian or some mongrel adaptation of both. Not an attempt to stereotype gay men. It was just that Derek was knowledgeable where things artistically decorative were concerned. Having thought that, I thought what did I know about any of the aforethought. Precious little.

Ambience reigned supreme. An adapted floorplan ran two rooms lengthwise, side by side, divided by sets of french doors beneath circular fanlight decor. The doors were open to ease the traffic overflow of Christmas diners, and to present to full advantage the inn's gleaming wood panels, snowy white and sparkling table settings, and the overall bedecked with boughs, holly, and mistletoe, to a falalalalah extravanganza. Fireplaces on either room's outside walls, burned yule logs brightly drawing attention to brick hobs, marble surrounds, and carved mantelshelves. Wherefrom, of course, dangled scarlet felt stockings. Despite these images from childhood, I knew in a flash that preschool male children were not welcome in this multi-star restaurant.

The Maitre-d' scanned his leather-bound reservations list an unpardonably long time. Hoping against hope that he could rightfully deny us entry by lack of being on the list? Too bad for him. The Saddles had reserved a table for ten. A bleak grimace of defeat accompanied the man's self-important,

"Ah, yes. The Saddle party. Right this way."

The kiddy highchairs were trendy, but a big mistake. No trays fronted them. They had to be pushed smack up against the table's edge, where they put their occupants within reach of assorted taboo items. Their low chair arms necessitated a snugly fastened safety belt. The deprivation/motivation theory was reaffirmed once again. Take a perpetual motion toddler, tie him to squeezed immobility, and the result is a writhing little person struggling to be free. Unless someone keeps him amused. With small squeaky toys brought along. Allowed to handle unbreakable utensils. Has salt shaken on his palm to taste with the tip of his tongue. Using foil-wrapped butter pats for mini building blocks. All this frenzied creativity creating havoc with the amuser's (moi) attempts at unflapability. Ten years later, the later guests straggled in.

Mater, Pater, Mary Jane and Ma and Pa, arrived in one group. Another fifteen minutes form Hell ticked by as we waited for Mary Jane's new friend from AA to make his appearance. He turned out to be a no-show. Would it have been too much to expect that this interim could have been put to good use in menu selection preferences, rather than consoling Mary Jane's constant jitters with asinine reasons for the drunk's non-appearance? (By that time I was calling it the way I saw it) Our waiter sided with me. He opened Mrs. Saddle's carte du jour and presented it to her.

Mater, ever predictable, declared all three choices looked so nice, so would the waiter take the other guest's orders first. The waiter's gaze shifted to Pater Saddle. He promptly went for the roast standing rib, bless him, then ruined my admiration for his decisiveness by delaying the waiter with umpteen questions: was an outside cut possible, was it real Yorkshire pudding or the Americanized popover, were the potatoes roasted around the joint or baked separately? I considered Ma and Pa's instant echo of his choice a fish-out-of water response. Mary Jane didn't want anything. On the spot, a fast interjection from me, "Duckling l'Orange, please." John picked up on the cue sent him, swiftly put in his request for the broiled salmon. All orders taken, right? Wrong.

An argument ensued between Mary Jane and her mother. The mother coaxed and cajoled her daughter to at least have a salad. The waiter, as eager as I was to get on with it, suggested the house vegetarian offering. It came with steamed vegetables atop a bed of pasta topped with the chef's special sauce. He lost my esteem when he went on to name each vegetable distinctly, and the five cheeses used for the sauce. Mary Jane didn't care for any of it. Mr. Saddle opined softly that she might like some of it when she saw it, and that the waiter should bring it for her to see. The waiter rolled his eyes heavenwards before he directed his orbs at me.

"And for the children?" Pencil at the ready.

No children's menu was available. I smiled, "We'll just share from our plates with them."

"There will be a charge, all the same."

Not wanting him to think we were paupers, "Do you have fish sticks or french fries?"

Offended, indeed. "I am afraid not."

I shot him my best schoolmarm disciplinary stare. "Do you have child portions of anything?"

Wounded. "I could ask the chef." Addressed Mr. Saddle. "Some wine while you wait?"

Mr. Saddle surprised the heck out of the snooty waiter. Authoritative commission, "Pinot gris, I think. One from an Oregon winery, if you have it."

In the waiter's eyes, he had somewhat redeemed us, "Excellent choice, Sir."

A busboy topped up our water glasses. Mary Jane had emptied hers. A Mid-West version of a sommelier delivered the pinot gris to our table. He knew the drill. Presented the Label for Mr. Saddle's inspection. Uncorked the bottle. Decanted a splash for his approval sip. At the nod, filled each flute to the correct fraction. Mr. Saddle advised us to enjoy the wine's fragrance. Inhaled from his stemware in demonstration. My initial sniff reminded me of wildflowers and meadows. My second sniff smelled like shhh..! Acutally, that's what it was. An odor from one of Bobby's diaper destroying poopies. Diners at nearby tables caught the drift. Sought the source with looks askance.

From the looks of Mary Jane's upside down wine glass, a tacit agreement seemed to exist between herself, her parents, and AA. Another agreement existed between John and myself. If at a restaurant, washroom responsibility for Bobby was mine. For Benny, the onus rests upon John. I unhitched Bobby from his avante garde childchair, shouldered the compulsory adjunct to motherhood—the ubiquitous diaper bag, and with self-protective bated breath loped off to do my duty.

Benny did not approve my departure. His vocal dissent sent abroad a soundtrack that set a child abuse scenario. Ma, ever on the watch that her grandsons receive no cruel or unusual punishment, sprang to Benny's rescue. Released his seatbelt, stating her intent to carry him off to look out the windows to see if they could see any birdies. Goodies, shoesies, poopies, birdies, I felt sure that my children would suffer from some sort of language psycho-sies once enrolled in kindergarten. For the nonce, Ma had saved the peace. Pater Saddle slipped in the subject of his son's Shakespearean play, where he could get tickets, for what date. I cantered into the Ladies.

One more sign that children were out at the inn. No provision for diaper changing. Bobby was forced to lie on the powder room floor. Literally. No professional wrestler could have pinned him down more effectively. The effort expended to remove, wipe, and retape on a clean diaper while in this position, triggered sweat glands beneath my warmish Christmas sweater. Hair-do strands trickled down, too. Diaper disposal was a whole other problem. Single-handedly, because I had to keep Bobby captive with the other, I yanked off paper towelling yardage, wrapped up the jobbie, and crammed it into the dainty wastie baskie. I had done my best. Those waxy doodad stickups overperfuming the lavatory atmosphere were on their own.

Quite on her effortless own, Mater Saddle had reduced our waiter to a quivering nervous breakdown level, all the way down from his shirt-fronting jabot to his tight black trousered hauteur. Our entrees had arrived, and were set on an opened folding table awaiting distribution. Ma and Pa and Mr. Saddle had been duly served their roast beef platters. Before Mary Jane got her veggie mélange, Mrs. Saddle sweetly proclaimed,

"I have decided to have the salmon."

The waiter's oversight in failing to take her order at the proper time represented a flagrant breach in his etiquette repertoire. If pallor counted, the waiter might faint dead away. Having waitressed during my college years, I could guess the chef's temperamental reaction. His prima donna attitude had survived going to all the trouble of whipping up two plates for two children, little people with undeveloped palates and no discernment for cuisine, and now, the waiter would have to face him with forgotten order travesty. Big whoop! thought I. But in the busy-to-frantic kitchen, all Hell might break loose.

To give the devil chef and his sous-chef imps their due, the beef ala Wellingon was fit for a royal duke, The flakey pastry elicited an involuntary, "Upon my word!" from Pater at his first bite. He recognized genuinely roasted potatoes when he tasted them. My duckling melted in the mouth. Mrs. Saddle gamely buttered a croissant as a signal that we should all eat before our meals cooled. John cut up the children's turkey slices (shades of Thanksgiving past) and as far as I was concerned they could do whatever they liked with their mashed potatoes and peas. For delicious moments the whole twenty-mile trek, et al, seemed worth the effort.

I reached for a swallow of the pinot gris. My glass was empty. Mary Jane, seated to my right, regarded her vegetable heap in a smilingly smug inertia. At least she sat silent and no gays were present for her to insult. Mrs. Saddle's salmon was accepted with pleasure, no recriminatory grudge against the waiter. Her insipid nice's and good's gravelled me sometimes, but at that meal I sensed a strength in her. Dealing with an alcoholic offspring had to be a heartbreak. Any worse than coming to terms with accepting a homosexual son or daughter? For which there was no cure? Distancing oneself from the problem, the way Del's father had done, instead of desertion, the way Derek's father had decided upon?

Del. She had faced enough rejection. She deserved a reciprocal Christmas present. Brains wracked as to how and what. The palate-cleansing sherbert (British spelling in honour of of my recently acquired admiration for my mother-in-law) prolonged the boys contentment to sit still—ice cream to them-after the thrill of planting their peas into their mashed potatoes with no reprimand from anyone, conversation resumed in the pause between entrees and dessert courses. The Play was The Thing. John's parents exclaimed a how hard John must have worked and suggested that he and I take a real holiday at their expense during spring break. John's, "No way!" caught us all off guard. He had sent out resumés, had received offers. He had job interviews to attend. Long-range, he hoped to finish his thesis towards a doctorate, get into a four-year college system, sell or house and move into a safer school district for the boys. Talk about a total surprise! He had been doing all this without talking it over with me? I didn't mind his ambition, but sell our house so soon? I said so.

"Sell our house?"

"Sure. It's pretty well fixed up and we can make a good profit on it."

The prospect dismayed. Refused to sink in. I excused myself from the table to make a restroom retreat. Regained composure was defeated by wronged anger holding the emotional fort. Wouldn't I love to give John a dose of his own medicine? I would. I never did anything without consulting him first. Not even a credit card purchase. He deplored credit card charges. I suddenly knew how to kill two birds with one stone. At full height, I marched up to the matre-d's podium in the vestibule and charged a gift certificate, luncheon for two—covered Del and Les.

"The twenty-five dollar certificate, Madam?"

"Make it thirty-five. They might want dessert."

Dessert futher restored my equanimity. The men forked up strawberry/rhubarb pie. The women had gone for the trifle. Mary Jane had obviously found her appetite. She chowed down a trifle serving quick as cat can wink an eye, called loudly to the waiter to fetch second helping. The ingredients in English trifle included sponge cake soaked in sherry. Mary Jane knew that.

## XV

I knew that keeping a secret friendship with Del ranked, if not as a felony, it certainly qualified as an infraction of marriage vows ethics. I was much heartened in this clandestine plot by Ring Lardner's comment in his short story "Gullible's Travels", quote: If you can't break a promise you made to your own wife, what kind of promise can you break? Slightly twist Mr. Lardner's logic to fit the game I was playing, and it came around to a comforting: If you can't keep a secret from your own husband, what kind of secret can you keep?

Keeping the secret friendship was not put to the test right away. Benny's chicken pox claimed front and center stage. One blister appeared on his forehead near his hairline. My first assessment that he had burned himself was illogical because our old-fashioned steam radiators wore perforated, protective metal covers. Later, a change of his disposable Big Boy underpants exposed a dozen blisters in the warmer creases of his little body. He felt hot. Science has since found a way to take a child's temperature in his ear. Then, the thermometer went into an orifice that rhymed with ear. Benny and Bobby never succumbed to this procedure willingly. I passed on the emotional and physical struggle. The kid had a temperature. I called the pediatrics group of Drs. Liggett, Wilson, and Paine.

If the name fits. It was a pain in the neck to get past the receptionist. No matter what dire information one disclosed to the woman, she always punctuated the symptoms list with, "uhhu" . . . "Uhhu". . . the string followed always by the same question,

"Does he have a temperature?"

"Yes."

"What was the thermometer reading?"

"A hundred and one." An educated guess, but she didn't need to know that. Besides, I had learned that if a child doesn't have a temperature, the receptionist won't work him in between scheduled appointments.

A long pause. "Dr. Wilson might be able to see him between his two-thirty and three o'clock appointments."

I knew it would do no good to tell her that Benny had the chicken pox. Her stock reply, ever repeated to lay diagnoses,

"We won't know that until the doctor sees him."

The doc didn't get paid for telephone diagnosis, and he did not want to risk a lawsuit for malpractice. Fair enough if the illness was a complicated one. Daddy dear would have to come home early whether he had warned about personal calls to the college, or whether he liked it or not, or whether it was convenient or not.

It wasn't convenient. It inconvenienced the office staff to get him to the phone. It interrupted his teaching, and worse, the studies the students had to pay for. For the life of me, I couldn't recall a single instance when a professor apologized for cutting a class short and the students were in the least upset. Usually, it was the exact opposite. John was conscienteous about his work and about being a good father. He suggested Ma or Pa as chauffeur alternatives. No hope there. And I'd be darned if I let him off the hook by asking Del, since he had forbidden a friendship with her. John dropped everything and drove home in time to get Benny to the doctor's appointment on time.

Dr. Wilson was running late. What else was new? An hour and ten minutes dragged past while John held a whining Benny on his lap in a waiting room filled with contagious diseases. Into the examine-room progress. False optimism. Another fifteen minutes crawled by. Dr. Wilson slipped in, gave Benny a two-second eyeball scan, affirmed that Benny had the chicken pox. A prescription emulsion to desensitize inflamed nerve endings in the itchy skin areas. Tylenol for the fever. A stethoscope moment. I still think that aspirin got a bad rap publicity-wise in order to boost the sale of Tylenol. Read the small print. It has serious side-effect possibilities. I opted for baby aspirin. Cheaper. Our medical plan benefits from the college were thin. They did not cover office visits or prescription costs. I was even leery about dosing Benny with the emulsion. How did it know which nerve endings to numb? A skin neuron as opposed to a brain cell? The Surgeon General reports that AIDS may be transmitted only in a limited way. Then a doctor tells the Cracker Basket to lay off all gay employees in the food handling restaurant chain. Why? The high price of prescription medications by the pharmaceutical companies in the name of research. Negligence—the DPT shots that were a mortal risk for some babies longer than they should have been. Check the statistics at the Board of Health.

I had enough to worry about. My men had been gone a long

time. Apprehension niggled that Benny had a worse ailment than a childhood disease, although chicken pox has been re-evaluted as more than a skin problem, and rushed to a hospital. Meanwhile John crept homewards, bucking the rush-hour slowdown. Benny's screaming against his blister irritation, intensified by carseat incarceration, seared John's nerve endings to fever pitch. They arrived home definitely not happy. Enough said on the state they were in. I would have been happier if there had been less said, altogether.

Lucky John. He got to go to work. I bore the brunt of Benny's suffering symptoms and suffered through seven sleep-interrupted nights. Benny recovered to the leprosy-scab condition. Bobby's first blister hatched three days later. Chicken pox can have a three-week incubation period, and unborn babies can catch it from their affected mothers while still in the womb. I diagnosed Bobby for free. Strangely, he developed only one spot on his ankle, and one other in the crook of his elbow. They were pimply small. I covered them with two bandaids. Bobby loved that. My hat is off to whomever invented bandaids. A concealed booboo ceases to hurt. I believed his lesser reaction stemmed from the fact that he was still young enough to be receiving residual hormonal immune support from being breast fed. Science makes a claim for improved intelligence quotients for babies nursed by their mothers. I believe it.

Bobby recovered. I relaxed. John broke out. He hadn't had the pox as a child. Well, he had it then. Real bad. In and on every conceivable surface. Yep! There, too! Especially there. He broke down. The budget be hanged. He wanted help. John had no regular physician. I called my Gyn-Ob. John was the last person on earth she wanted in her pregnant women filled waiting room. She prescribed over the telephone. I don't know what the capsules were supposed to do. They did nothing for John. They didn't relieve the itching—or so he claimed. They did not hasten the run of the disease. They certainly did not improve his disposition. Adult chicken pox should be more accurately referred to as ostrich pox. Herpes related, it can be gravely serious. Didn't I know it! John's case nearly killed me.

A hundred years later, a day arrived when John awoke in better spirits. His good looks were spot encrusted, but he felt better. He showered and got dressed. Apologized for his grumpiness. He offered to mind the boys if I wanted a break away from the house. Did I? Is the pope catholic? I have wondered why he wears a skullcap very like a yarmulke. But to get out of the house? Yes! And double yes!

Where to go? What to do? With whom? The gift certificate to the Old Mill Road Inn! I had forgotten about it completely. For such a late Christmas gift I would not have blamed her if Del never spoke to me again. She answered the phone on its first ring. (waiting for a someone special to call?) She could be ready to go out to lunch in ten minutes. Her eagerness bespoke a loneliness. Some friend I had been during these past weeks of sickroom duty. I said I'd pick her up at the corner. She laughed.

"Sneaking around, are we? I love it!"

I dressed up my good jeans and turtleneck shirt with the upgrade of the Fair Isle sweater vest my parents had given me for Christmas-on top of the money for us. Del wore a navy jumper over a red silk blouse. Dress codes be damned, I thought we came across as just right for a country inn luncheon. The inn looked less formal, too. Gone were the ropings and tinsel. The Maitre d' (maitresse d'?) at the entry pulpit was a woman in a plain black dress and glasses that had a cord attached to them. Patrons sat at about half the tables in one room. The second room's french doors were closed. A slow day? Nevertheless, we were asked if we had reservations. We didn't. The woman raised her spectacles from the dangle position to a perched loftiness on the bridge of her nose. They aided her study of a page in the reservation book. They came off to enable her to scan the diningroom. In thorough encompassment.

"This way." No please?

Had it been my imagination, or had she also perused us as she took her time poring over the reservation list? Were we unsuitably dressed? Yikes! Did she think we were a 'couple'? Tall me in pants. Tiny Del in skirts? I felt miffed. How dared she? We reached a back table and the idea got shrugged off. Was the table's position significant? Not really. This often happened when there was no male escort. We haven't come such a long way, Baby. I knew that. A lot of women knew that.

One aspect of the inn remained the same. The waiter was a bit snooty, and the haute cuisine predominated in the consommé, the stir-fried Chinese vegetables with gingered chicken, and the creme brulée dessert. We ate with relish—the gusto kind, and happily sated, we sipped cappuccino and talked our heads off.

Traded information. Les was in California because she refused to live sponging off Del. Les was a skilled cook. In California, homosexuality did not preclude an applicant's success at being hired. The problem, believe it or not, was that Les was a woman competing in a man's field. She was attending a school in San Francisco to raise herself to chef status. To cheer away Del's loneliness, I related the chicken pox episodes, turning high anxiety travails into humorous anecdotes; itchy pimples on a penis, for example. Del appreciated the comedic side of it all, but she reminded me of how lucky I was to have Benny and Bobby, chicken pox or not.

"I know it. But I would have loaned then out these past few weeks."

Del's sadness returned. "One thing that bothers me a lot is that my father is so disappointed at no hopes of ever having a grandchild. Heartbroken, really."

I had heard this before. Why did Del keep harping on it? I made a try at steering the conversation to the negative side of raising children. Mentioned the problems my in-laws were having with Mary Jane. Wrong argument."

"Vickie, if I could change by going for counselling, or therapy, or to a support group, or climb twelve steps to normal, I would do it in a flash. I have agonized over my lot for years. I now accept it as cure-less. I just feel sorry for my father. I am all he's got. His whole life centered on me after my mother died. I can't imagine why God dealt him such a low blow. Now he thinks that his hopes of immortality by way of grandchildren have been denied him too. That's the worst part.

A non sequitor? I glanced around to signal the waiter to bring our check. My eyes lit upon a table for two, the two diners silhouetted against a window with a view. Did a double take. There sat Mary Jane across from a young man. A stand supported an ice bucket from which protruded a bottle-green, narrow neck. Our check arrived as I checked an impulse to wave. I presented the gift certificate. The waiter carried it away. The Maitresse d', eyeballs aimed at us over the top of her glasses, trotted the gift certificate back. Stiff upper lip informed me that the certificate should have been presented when we came in.

Asked a stupid question, "What difference did that make?"

Pear-shaped tones, "It is customary to so do."

Meekly, "I am sorry. I'll certainly so do the next time."

Not satisfactory, "I'm sure you will, but I cannot accept the certificate for this meal. It will cause problems with the computer."

That little shrimp of a Del leapt to her feet. Told the maitresse d's chest, "It's the certificate or nothing!"

I stood to support her Hobson's choice. Del wrapped her arm around my waist.

"Come on, Darling. Let's go home!"

Crossing the parking lot, Del told me not to look like I looked. I knew how I looked. A cross between outrage and incredulity.

"Why did you do that? . . . put your arm around me..and.. Did your want her to think that we are..we are..

"She already thought we were. Take it from me, Vickie, when a persecuted section of any population can laugh at itself, it is halfway home to defeating the persecutors. Why do you think there are so many Jewish comedians?"

"You thought that woman's attitude was funny?"

"Sure. Think about it. If you saw it in a movie you would laugh."

Del was right. The holier-than-thou expression on that rouged face was funny. I smiled at the image it conjured up. Del giggled. She approved me in a faked superiority act.

"That is more like it. It is very much better to so do!"

Teary-eyed laughing hysteria lasted sporadically all the way home. I dropped Del off at her drivewyay. I didn't care who saw us. Del's parting sally,

"We've got to keep meeting like this. Next time I'll buy the gift certificate."

John met me right behind our front door. His chicken pox irritation seemed to have attacked him in a relapse. He was barely able to state his case.

"My sister called."

"So?"

"You know what so!"

The awful truth dawned. That little fink had ratted on me. I wouldn't have ratted her fall off the wagon. The little doublecrosser. One of Ring Lardner's baseball players, Alibi Ike, said it, "I would of been okay if not for that."

## XVI

Okay. I was not totally okay with the inn fiasco. It bugged me that the hostess had jumped to the conclusion that Del and I were Lesbians. Was it our clothing? Surely, jeans and jumpers don't denote homosexuality. Was it the tall and short stature? I didn't go for assumption that either of us looked mannish. Shades of Sappho! Had the woman thought we were lovers at her first sight of us? I tried to come to terms with how I felt about that. It's one thing to be tolerant unto magnanimous when the aberrant behaviour has no direct bearing on one's own life. It is a whole other kettle of fish to step into another's shoes and get to know a smidgen of how it feels to live with a societal stigma. I confess to my discredit, I didn't like to be tagged, even erroneously, as a lesbian. If I continued to be seen with Del would I run this risk, and could I deal with it?

    Love tokens began slipping through the letterbox slot set in the old-fashioned door of a past era. Mater and Pater Saddle, ever British justice fair, mailed the same Valentine to each grandson. It was a rockinghorse cut-out wearing a heart-shaped saddle. Enfolded was a check to be banked towards future college tuition. It was a relief to find no card from Del on the hall mat, a card to somehow explain. Ma and Pa set florist flowers attached to floaty balloons for Benny and Bobby, and foil-wrapped heart-shaped, chocolate candies for us all to share. It was a stretch to even think Del might send flowers to get me in trouble. Why had I entertained the slightest worry about that? John bought his sweetheart a shiny bag filled with baby Snicker bars. He knew I enjoyed them. I ate one immediately and almost stopped worrying. Two cards came from Benny and Bobby. Mailed by their father. A thoughtful gesture. Except the sight of them as they came through the slot, a first-time surprise, generated a heart palpitation or two.

Valentine's Day came and went. How stupid can you get? I felt a silly ass, a fool. Del wasn't interested in me as anything more than a friend and neighbor. I knew that. I had always known that. The next time I was with her, and I had decided there would be a next time, if anyone so much as looked at us sideways, or cast aspersions about queer couples, I planned to ask that snot if he or she wanted to make something out of it! What we think about ourselves is what matters. Wasn't that a better role model for my sons than shunning people who were considered different from us? I determined it was.

Had God decided to call me on it? On February sixteenth a pink, large, square envelope slid through the letterbox slot. God, was this some kind of test? If so, I was on the verge of failing it. John beat me to it. He handed it to me. He had glimpsed the Mr. and Mrs. addressees and gallantly handed the envelope over that I might have the honor of opening it. It was an invitation to Uncle Victor and Zelda's wedding, set for April the first, April Fools' Day. I felt foolish. No sooner had I resolved no more apologies where my friendship with Del was concerned, than I went into a tizzy over a pink envelope. Enough was enough. To myself I reaffirmed my 'yeah, do you want to make something out of it?' should any jerk dare to criticize my friendship with any person I darned well chose to make friends with.

I resolutely set about renewing the kaffeeklatsch ritual with Del. A coverup makeup base lotion on John's pox traces restored his self-image sufficiently to send him forth on his appointed rounds in the classrooms. His absence left me free to call Del. I called every day for two weeks. On the days when spring seemed just around the corner, the boys and I interrupted our strolls to ring her doorbell. A nobody home aura emanated from the house next door. The wooden railing geese stuck out as a flock all forlorn awaiting their mistress's safe return. My guess was that Del was visiting Leslie. I hoped so.

Love was in the air, but Zelda forbade us to give her a bridal shower. She should have saved her breath. A Genoese family brooked no such negligence on its part. The surprise was that the suprise shower was held at Zelda's sister's house. Anna impressed me as a younger and sister similar, a Zelda who had allowed herself to get out of shape. The bogeyman of giving birth to five children will get your figure if you don't watch out. Everyone had chipped in towards the decorations and the food. No one was expected to be weight watching on the shower evening. Mary Jane excepted. She never seemed to eat much.

No trick games. No loud music. No male stripper. Only traditional trappings and nothing intended to bring a blush to even the most virginal bride-to-be.

The buffet hodge-podge reflected the donating guests' personalities. Ma delivered home-baked tarts: pasticciotti (vanilla custard and pineapple fillings), crosticciotti (a sweetened cheese inside), and pasta frolla crusts enriched with a paste made from dried citrus fruits. Mater Saddle had performed her adroit sidestep with a raspberry flan beneath a white and dark chocolate glaze with 'ordered from a gourmet catalogue' written all over it. Tube cookies from the dairy case to slice and bake told it the way it was with yours truly. Mary Jane had tossed in a couple of pounds of Godiva chocolates—liqueur filled. Anna had chopped up raw vegetables served with a dip and crackers. Zelda must had brewed the tea and coffee. They tasted too good to be true.

A learning experience for Mater Saddle if she was paying attention.

As many synonyms as ever were invented flowed forth as the unwrapped boxes revealed lingerie, Lenox candy dishes, a carry-on luggage bag with wheels, feathery mules, a handpainted scarf, two throw-away cameras, and the fun present of the night—a pair of silk pajames monogrammed 'Hers' on the top, and 'His' on the pajama bottoms Lovely. Pretty. Exquisite. These rolled right over Mr. Saddle's head, but we all had to agree with her when she said that Zelda was such a nice person. We knew she meant it in all that 'nice' encompasses. To be in Zelda's company boosted the way one felt about oneself. Zelda's rare talent kept the guests blithely chatting and having a good time. Had I caught the shadow of a smile on Mary Jane's lips? If so, Zelda had performed a miracle.

A miracle impossible—if Del and Les were ever allowed a legal wedding ceremony. Evidently, they considered themselves lifetime partners dedicated to each other. A movement was afoot in Hawaii to pass a law to allow same-sex marriages. It didn't seem to be anywhere near a reality. One more social-outcast cross for homosexuals to bear, shrugged I. It was a contemplation too deep for a person enjoying four hours freedom from child care and domesticity.

A personal problem closer to home had to be solved, and that right early. I had to come up with a babysitter to take care of Benny and Bobby if, and when, John and I were to attend Uncle Victor and Zelda's wedding ceremony and reception. I couldn't round up the usual prospects because any eligible candidate was also on the guest list. The three Saddles, as my in-laws, were automatically included as family in Uncle Victor's eyes. Any discernable activity in the house next door would have raised my hopes, always supposing I could hold a discussion on the subject in a manner pragmatic enough in presentation to avoid overheated debate. I decided to wait. To give John a chance to solve the sitter problem. He deserved that chance, didn't he? If he came up empty, then, and only then would I suggest our neighbor for the job.

I turned down John's immediate response whereby his mother would be only too glad to hire a sitter for us, on the grounds that accepting her largesse undermined our determination to stand on our own two financial feet. Plus, our children left in charge of a total stranger left me cold to the idea. His querie, "How about a friend of Mary Jane's?" got snipped in the bud by the grim reaper horror spread across my face. The problem pended while John sought a solution among his students. Easter break was about to scatter John's disciples far and wide into part-time jobs or off to Florida. My come-back-little-Sheba mantra went into overdrive. Del did come home. Through the round window halfway up our stairway shone midnight headlights. The Ancients knew how to evoke power. I mentally thanked them for sharing it with me.

Del filled my coffee cup and filled me in on California. Les chopped salads, temporarily. Her cookery classes, taught by a prestigious institution, guaranteed her a job following graduation. The Cracker Basket showed signs of settling the class action suit. As in most class action suits, the lawyers would get the lion's share, and the restaurant chain insisted that the incident remain sub rosa if money changed hands, but the litigants would get satisfaction in winning the suit as well as some dwindle-down funds. Did Del intend to move to California? Good news. Not for at least a year. Benny watched video cartoons. Bobby lay on his back in a dedicated study as to what was keeping Del's front, middle, sofa leg attached to the sofa. What good children they were being! I grasped the moment to broach the sitter request. Del agreed providing it was okay with John.

"Not to worry. He is desperate."

Moved right along to the what to wear dilemma. Del came up with a solve.

"Shop from a catalogue."

Catalogues had only just begun their mail invasion. They were too fat to go through our mail slot so they were left on the front porch. Electronic shopping. I could do that. I could do that by lifting one finger to dial a toll-free number. A dress of my choice would be delivered to the house.

Bobby delivered the front middle leg of Del's couch to us coffee drinkers. Del thought it was cute. Hugged Bobby and said how very much she wanted a little boy in her house to take the legs off things. This brought the talk around to adoption and sperm banks and the difficulties involved when Homosexuals made efforts to have a child to raise. Del and Les had done their homework. Explored every option and avenue. Del sighed.

"All it would take is just one tiny drop of sperm."

Seeking to lighten what was turning into a sad situation, "Gosh, we toss out more sperm than that at least a couple of times a week!"

Del did not find it funny. "Do me a favor. Toss some of it in my direction."

'Favor' activated a promise stored in the old brain box. It went something like—if ever Del asked a favor, and there she sat asking a favor, maybe facetiously, but asking it all the same. My answer stunned her.

"Okay. I'll see what I can do."

Del had reminded me to get real. I restated my intention. There was no harm in thinking about it, was there? A fallacious premise if ever here was one. Hadn't Einstein's thinking evolved the equation from whence came the atomic bomb?

I expected there would be problems, but what man's (or woman's) mind can conceive, and all the rest of that maxim . . . . 'Conceive'. Certainly the operative concept for this project to succeed.

## XVII

Yogi Berra's enigmatic advice, "When you come to a fork in the road, take it!" didn't come across as such a crazy idea when I found myself in a similar 'Y' sort of situation. One prong led to keeping my promise to Del. The other prong meant staying on very friendly terms with John if I was to get the goods to deliver. A husband whose views on friendship with Del leaned towards hostility. Common sense recommended I set a position as close as possible to the crotch of the configuration, thus avoiding getting too far out on a limb in either direction. Hopefully, the goal as seen from this vantage point, would stand as a constant reminder of 'why' I was doing something so nuts in the first place.

Help came from an unexpected source. John relented on his hardcore antipathy towards Del. Having exhausted himself in his failed sitter hunt, he was ready to listen when I suggested meekly that Del might consent to mind our children, but only if he thought it would be okay with him. His acceptance conditions I accepted with a grain of salt. The boys would have to be bathed and pajama-ed before we left so that any nudity would be circumvented. A timely arrival for the wedding meant our departure at three o'clock. A brief recapitulation on pajamas so early persuaded the mother in me of there being no harm wearing pajamas with feet in them in the late afternoon. I accidentally on purpose refrained from mentioning diaper changes. The sitter problem was settled, and John's attitude towards Del softened.

So far so good. One serious hurdle remained. Getting possession of the sperm. Our birth control method included a spermicidal lubricant on a condom. Double insurance against another 'accident'. I definitely did not want any more children. A bit risky, but I told John that the lubricant was irritating and could we stop using it for awhile? No argument there. The second part was a stickler. What person, and why, would any lunatic be collecting used condoms? Stalemated. Every avenue explored put me in check.

Other things had to be considered. It became urgent to check the catalogues I had been hoarding to find a new dress. Piled on the bed, the glossies looked formidable. Benny napped, but for some reason Bobby stayed wide awake. I carted him into my bedroom lest he disturb his brother. He played happily at trying to find a way to remove the staples holding the booklets together. The prices absorbed my complete attention. Our budget rule of thumb required discussion on any purchase exceeding one hundred dollars. The dress ordering had been put off until there was no time for that. Delivery took up to ten days. Into a second hour search, a basic shirtwaist with bright navy stripes, with a lemon yellow, sleeveless bolero jacket, attired a model who had my coloring. She looked the way I always wanted to look. Classically comfortable. Getting through to an order taker, providing credit card numbers, garment numbers, price charge numbers, size numbers, and address numbers, asked for by 'Bonnie', served to keep my mind off Bobby's too-quiet preoccupations. The toilet's constant flushing swishes infiltrated as white background noise, an irrelevancy to a mind bent on searching through jewel boxes and drawers in an accessories search to complement the new dress. Bobby toddled over to join me as a closet exploration yielded up zilch in the way of suitable shoes. He seemed to have sprung a leak. A leak! Somewhere, water gurgles persisted in the way a certain dog persists in novels, as in 'somewhere a dog barked'.

The bathroom! My toilet bowl overflowed! Flooded the floor and rose steadily to the doorstep height leading into the upper hall. Wedging the toilet tank ball up with my slipper shut the intake valve off. Every towel in the linen closet went as sacrifices towards a fast absorbent action to save the kitchen ceiling below the tiled floor. A napless Bobby soon tired of watching his mother wipe up and wring out water into the bathtub. He beat a retreat back to the bedroom where he fell asleep on the bedspread among a little boy blue haystack of loose catalogue pages. He didn't react one whit to removal of soaked clothing and a lift to a dry spot on the bed. He was out for the count. Flushing pages and pages down the poor old toidie (Gramma's word for it) had tuckered him out completely.

John plunged. No man had ever plunged more assiduously. Whatever blocked the plumbing refused to be budged. I had taken the plunge on charging a ninety-eight-dollar dress, plus handling and shipping fees, no tax as the company was out of state, a small consolation that would carry no exculpatory weight with a husband who kept repeating,

"How did you let this happen. For crying in a bucket, how did you let this happen?"

I decided that telling him about the dress could be postponed for as long as its delivery would take—ten days. Telling my beloved that we needed a plumber immediately had to be faced up to. Another dozen non-productive plunger attacks and John surrendered his suction cup. And since the whole mess was my fault, it behooved me to find the number that called the plumber.

I spoke to yellow-page plumbers. Right up to the end of the business day and on into the twenty-four hours a day service promisers. One condescended to arrive within twenty-four hours. Translated: sometime the following morning. I will spare the details of how we made it through the night. My main maternal fear hovered around how Benny's toilet training might be affected. Maybe a lifetime trauma. So much written information was available on psychological damage hinging on toilet training techniques.

What with his fifty-dollar knock on the front door, and his twenty dollars for every hour thereafter, parts extra, the plumber unhinged my cerebral equilibrium. He instructed me to fill a few pots with water in case he had to shut off the water at the main. One fleeting glance into the toilet tank, and yep, he had to shut off the water at the main. He shook his head as he returned my soggy slipper to my custody. As God is my witness, never will I buy another house with only one bathroom.

Del was in the same boat. Fortunately, her one was not leaking. She shared it with us for five hours, back and forth as demand arose, Benny fooling me just for the fun of a quick dash to DeeDee's. Was it unfair to say the hours were stretched to an even five, a five that multiplied the twenty bucks to an even one hundred? To be fair, the plumber had not stopped for lunch. Also, the rusted basement pipes had resisted wrenchings at their old joints. Yeah. The man had earned his pay.

So, just as I was appreciating his skill, did he have to cast a slur at his departure? As if I hadn't known that Sears Catalogues were okay in outhouse days, but not in inside flushers.

"Ma'am, reg'lar toilet paper is better-suited to indoor plumbing."

The new fitting numbers gave John no joy. He wanted to know what had caused the malfunction in case it happened again. I assured him that it would never happen again. The lie lay in saying this information came straight from el plumbo's mouth. Evasion not accepted. What, exactly, had caused the flood? Some creativity required. It took a suspicious minute or two.

"Well? For Pete's sake! For this kind of money don't tell me we didn't get any answers!"

Throat clearing, "we-ell, it seems that these older houses still have some lead in their pipes, and . . . and it sometimes plays havoc with the water flow."

John not only bought it, he said he remembered hearing about how lead used to be put in pipes long ago. Was it dangerous? Was it okay for us to drink the water?

"Of course. Don't worry. The plumber took care of everything."

Interrogation over. Wasn't I lucky to live with a man who was working on his thesis towards a PhD, who was also so naive as to swallow the water explanation? On the other hand, John had no shortage in the smarts department. Maybe he had come to Yogi Berra's fork in the road, too, and had been wise enough to take the easier way out.

# XVIII

Salad days. The days when no matter what went into the toss, this college student could sort it out. Even tried her had at writing poetry, a line of which returned to haunt me, "Cruel the wasp-wasted hourglass jar". Ten days had elapsed and the dress from the catalogue company remained a no-show. Three more days and the denim skirt and a tank top combo was going to a wedding. It was time to remind 'Work & Play, Inc.' that it was remiss in its delivery promise.

BettySue identified herself by name on the 800 number line. She was super polite.

"The company does do its very bayest to get their clothes out on time. They send it priority mail, but that don't mean it gets there no faster. I am sorry."

Despite a few mistakes in grammar, BettySue was correct. A check with the post office confirmed that the word 'priority' as in 'priority mail' bore no relationship to its etymology. The cliffhanger countdown continued. A clue on the toll this interim suspense took—the boys began giving me a wide berth and sat atypically subdued at mealtimes. Another clue. John began working on his thesis into the small wee hours.

Wake up time. My men should not have to suffer for something that was not their fault. Retribution demanded bedtime stories, and extra time set aside for extra hugs. For John, no matter how late the hour, his bedtime would include a wife who was in the mood if he was in the mood.

"The House That Jack Built", in pictue book form, started off my good intentions. First page illustration exposed for viewing. Text,

"This is the house that Jack built."

Audience interruption, "Is Jack Daddy?"

Benny had remembered that John's father sometimes called his son 'Jack' when his wife was out of hearing.

"This man has the same name as Daddy. People named John are called Jack sometimes."

"Why?"

Benny had me there. "I don't know why, Honey. They just are." Bobby surprised the heck out of us. "Me know."

"You do? Tell us why."

"Toz its nice."

Sidebar flash. Egads! Mrs. Saddle had passed her adjective limitations along in the genes.

As the story progressed, another realization materialized The tale about the house that Jack built was rife with sex and violence. It contained a malt-stealing rat, a rat-killing cat, a cat-hating dog, a dog-kicking cow, scenes of violence, all. As for sex, try this on for metaphor. A maiden all forlorn, who milked the cow with the crumpled horn, then kissed the man all tattered and torn. Historical fact; nursery stories were not the innocents they pretended to be. I skipped past the priest and the reversed order sequence back to the house that Jack built, to an ad lib ending that they all lived happily ever after.

The sudden ending bothered the children only because they did not want to give up my attention so easily. Most mothers think their children are smart. Mine were. They had figured out how to stretch the bedtime ritual if they begged to see the stars. The night sky fascinated us. They knelt on the window seat to behold what lit the darkness. The moon played peek-a-boo, the March wind clouds hiding its face, then puffed away to let our friend shine at us again. No stars. We looked and looked. We had almost given up when Bobby's sharp eyes espied one distant twinkler. The bold Venus? Nothing would do then but we had to say our song.

"Starlight, star bright/First star I see tonight/I wish I may, I wish I might/Have the wish I wish tonight."

We repeated it once more with feeling. Man! I hoped that Jiminy Cricket told the truth when he promised that when you wish upon a star, your wish comes true. In which event, my dress would be sure to arrive on the morrow.

If you haven't tried it, don't knock it. It worked. The agony of the wait ended the next day. The son of an elderly neighbor living to our right, delivered it with apologies. The postal service, unable to put such a large package through the mail slot, and loathe to leave it exposed on the front porch, had asked his mother to accept the shipment. A mother who had senior moments. The event slipped her mind. There I had been muttering blasphemies against the dress company, the post office, and computer communication systems. Son of a . . . gun!

I needed human input. I wore the dress over to Del's. Her opinion. The navy stripes against the white shone bright and 'springy', and the yellow bolero jacket enhanced my coloring. The full skirt allowed for a bit of a swirl in dancing. I whirled around with a pretend partner. Del advised me to calm down and have some coffee. Oxymoron advice? Have some caffeine and calm down? I guess it made sense, at that.

Benny and Bobby perked up at the introduction to the new kitten Les had given Del. It had flown with her from California in a carrier beneath her seat. The in-house, older cat, had assumed a protective role relationship with the newcomer. Her tail tip flipped agitated signals. Les had hoped that the baby kitty would make Del a little less lonely. I felt an underlying innuendo. Homosexual pairings keenly felt the deprivation of the bonding that shared child raising forges. A pretty picture. Del surrounded by two toddlers, a playful kitten, and a watchful, matronish cat. Wholesome joy depicted, if you asked me.

God, it is written, decreed a time for everything. Time's sobriquet is Father Time. Was that related to a woman's time limit in which to bear children? While a man may sire children ad finitum? Do maternal longings receive short shrift? My college days poem had been wise beyond my years. Time's passing can sting cruelly. Tempus was fugiting all over the place.

I continued to fail to find a chink in my stonewalled brain strain to give Del a chance, before it was too late, to get pregnant. I began to feel that it was not nice to fool Mother Nature. She was ruthless. I fought against my despair of ever outwitting her.

# XIX

Weddings are turning points. Their formalities can't help but promote than as sentient turning points. They bring an awareness that the union of two people and two families make for conscious change in lives. Other turning points pivot around a speck so seemingly trivial, that the astronomical changes inherent in them pass unnoticed at that point in time. I had come within a hair's breadth of missing a clue in my desperation to find opportunity's window in the stone wall.

Uncle Victor and Zelda were wed on April Fools' Day in the candlelit chapel. Zelda did not belong to the catholic church. Some guests were moved to tears. Some to smiles. Maybe a few took stock of their lives to date. Future spouses are met at weddings, 'tis said. While the I do's were vowed, John reached over and held my hand. A romantic touch. A reaffirmation of why I wore a gold wedding band.

The bride wore a pale gold suit. A vee insert of pleats fannning open and closed in a back interest as she walked down the aisle on Derek's arm. She carried red roses, what else? Uncle Victor stood for Tradition with a capital 'T'. The absence of a hat hinted at Zelda's independent nature. The baby breath sprigs tucked into her french twist, to me, betokened her willingness to compromise.

Zelda's son gave the bride away. Derek looked sensational in his tuxedo. Hair styled to fall into place no matter what the head toss. I caught a quick intake of breath from a male sitting across the aisle from us, evident attraction in his appraisal of Derek. I wished someone would explain to me how he knew that Derek was gay. Remember my reference to people finding partners at weddings? That young man recognized a possible sexual partner when he saw one. How? By what silent signal? John was no numbskull, yet he hadn't perceived the slightest notion of Derek's homosexuality. They had worked together, cheek by jowl for a whole month. Uncle Victor's best man, his foreman Ed Green, was trying for a surreptitious underhand of a passed hankie to the groom. No man in the chapel was more totally male than Uncle Victor. Ed Green's move was about as secret as a cat among the pigeons. Empathetic smiles came to the faces seeing a tear on Uncle Victor's cheek. No ridicule. What if it had been Derek who had wept openly? A different reaction? Uncle Victor and Zelda were pronounced man and wife.

The married couple retired behind a screen to sign the register. I was left to my strange thoughts. Homosexuals were human beings. The bride and groom reappeared, the bride on the groom's arm. They were introduced for the first time as Mr. and Mrs.

And, to the jaw-dropping startlement of embarrassment of the Traditionalist, as has become the latter-day custom, everyone who had witnessed the nuptials gave the pair a round of applause.

There came a pause in the guests' occupations, familiarly known as the Kodak and reception line moments. An hour or so when guests ramble the rented hall, sip drinks, and put on a bonhomie front while wondering how soon do we eat. Uncle Victor knew a lot of people. His guest list had run to well over a hundred family, friends, and business acquaintances. The caterers grew antsy before they received the nod to serve the vittles. Luckily, they were worth waiting for and restored the celebration to jovial. The host couple sat. The guests politely did likewise. Limbo was over, as it has been over also in the afterdeath precepts in a certain religion, joining the exclusion of equally terrifying practices; bloodletting, the murder of virgins, human sacrifice cruelty. A step in the right direction. This I believed in. Now, if we could only accept all human beings as valuable. I believed that would be good, too.

Round tables encircled, in concentric circles, the circular dance floor. Upon a raised platform waited a set of drums, skeletal music stands, and seven chairs. A piano rippled. The pianist knew her stuff. Her melodies were smoothing out the rustle, stir, and crowd hubbub without drowning out attempts at conversation. Sweet and Low. Which reminded me we were ingesting far too much sugar. The band filed in. I figured we could dance it off.

Our table seated us immediately to the right of the head table. Protocol, as we were important people to the bride and groom. Ma and Pa, the three Saddles, us, and the fellow who had gasped as Derek escorted his mother towards the altar. To whom was he important? Something arrived to take my mind off that subject. What? Oh, yes. I went bananas over the bananas Foster. Bananas flambéd in rum, drenched in liquid chocolate, enriched by whipped and ice cream, and a fresh giant strawberry garnish. Mary Jane took a few stabs at her bananas and left them lying wounded to give her full attention to the non-stop talker, Gordon (the gasper).

He held her by the ear the minute he mentioned his horse that he kept stabled in Concord Township. Had he knowingly chosen that subject because of his super sensitivity as a gay? Weren't gays notorious for their sensitivity? If he was gay. Or was he a natural psychic? If you have ever wondered what actress could play Maris on the Frasier show, Mary Jane would win out over any other auditioner. But Gordon had wrought a change. There she was, energized, animated, revealing her knowledge of, and devotion to horses. As a child she had had a pony.

Did I hear a laugh? Brief, but it might have been. Her brother John had been afraid of it. Was that why John kept Ruff-Ruff at arm's length and called him my dog? A phobia. Like suspicion of strangers and wary of casseroles? A reason for his homophobia? Carrying the idea a bit far, was I. Gordon probably was Mary Jane's date. He certainly knew how to hold her interest. Toast time. Ed Green, the best man, latched right onto the April Fools' date for the wedding. His speech was filled with good humored roasting. In summation,

"A man would have to be a fool not to woo and wed this very lovely lady." Glasses clinked.

Uncle Victor led his lovely lady out onto the dance floor. The band gave out with 'I'll be loving you always . . ." Couples joined them in the waltz.

A fool on Fools' Day, me. In the ladies' room I ventured a hint to Mary Jane that maybe Gordon was gay. I meant it as a warning because she was showing signs of falling for the guy. I started out hesitantly.

"Uh, how well do you know Gordon?"
Mary Jane had an I.Q. off the charts. No fooling around the point for her.

"Do you mean do I know that he's gay?"

Took the wind out of my sails. "Oh. . . . you know."

"You ninny! Everyone knows. Take a look at him, for God's sake!"

See. There it was again. The idea that one just had to look at him. I couldn't tell for sure just by looking at him. And I didn't chum up to the idea of being called a 'ninny'. What was that, anyway? The British form of nincompoop? I tried to one-up my sister-in-law.

"I think he likes Derek."

As if making an explanation to an idiot, "Everyone likes Derek."

"Well, you remember Derek is one, too."

"Have you been living in a cave or something? Who doesn't know that? And Gordo is my friend. He is the best friend I ever had. He's smart. He listens. He has a wonderful sense of humor. It's a relief to be in a man's company without the everpresent pressure of sexual overtones. So much the better for Derek if Gordo is his friend!"

Everpresent Sexual pressure got to me. A sample of British hyperbole? Or an imagination gone haywire? I couldn't recall any man who had dated Mary Jane more than once, and whatzisname had been a no-show at the Christmas dinner. My hand ceased applying a lipstick overload long enough for a pertinent impertinence.

"Pardon me? Weren't you the one who was against homosexuals at Thanksgiving? Who called John to tell him I was out with a lesbian?"

"See, Vickie? If you had the intelligence to see things clearly, and think things through, you wouldn't always be flying of the handle about nothing!"

Deserted, I considered Mary Jane's farewell statement. Decided it was false. I further consoled myself with the conjecture that she wasn't so smart after all. she had split an infinitive. So there!

It took no Einstein to figure that the powder room colloquy had done zilch to strengthen any bonding between Mary Jane and me. My self esteem sank to an idiotic also-ran slinking back to the family table. Asked John,

"How would you feel about dancing with a birdbrain who has been relegated to a short-tempered hermit living in a cave with only two small boys for company?"

John likes my sense of humor. Sometimes it catches him off guard. It took him a second or two, then he smiled.

"Does that mean you wanna dance, Baby?"

We tripped our light fantastic two step that we use to every rhythm from fox trot to samba, for a few bars. The bandleader announced Uncle Victor's request for a tango. A tango is one dance that defeats the two step. If Uncle Victor wanted a tango, it was his wedding, and I supposed he was entitled to tango. The showoff. Zelda's jacket removed, revealed an expanse of attractive back and firm bared arms. Those arms were not the arms of a woman past menopause, or as Erma Bombeck said it, arms that turn overnight into a perfect fit for dolman sleeves. Jealousy assailed me. Would my nose be out of joint as Uncle Victor's favorite child if he and Zelda had a baby?

I was only human. A little jealousy assailed me.

The whole room cleared the dance floor and watched as the pair strutted cheek-to-check, snapped into reverse, every bit of fancy footwork accented by the flair and flip of the rear pleats in Zelda's skirt. Sometimes a feeling overcame me that Uncle Victor was George Raft reincarnated. The quick whirls made me dizzy. At that moment I passed a turning point. So fast that the sensation left me even more lightheaded. I knew how to get possession of the sperm to give Del a chance to get pregnant.

'Goodnight Ladies', played by the band, ended the evening. Swaying together rhymically at the end of the party is a sort of foreplay. All cosied up together, I asked John if he liked my new dress. I felt his nod against my cheek. The confessed cost of it put air between us as John performed a hesitation step. I didn't know he could do that. Got back in contact as if John had decided this was not a good time for argument. I said I was sorry about the plumber's bill. Told him the plumber's advice to avoid future troubles. That we should only flush the youknow usual stuff down the toilet. Truth. Truth manipulated, not the you-know, condoms.

The dancing stopped. "What the heck am I supposed to do with them, then?"

On purpose—prolonged his suspense over a possible no-sex scenario, "Well . . . we could keep a supply of ziplock baggies in the nightstand . . . and just put the you-know in one until I could throw it out in the morning. Or whenever."

Turning point accomplished. All systems were not 'go'. The sperm had to be delivered while it was still viable. How long did sperm remain viable in a ziplock baggie? What was the best temperature for it? I had read about frozen sperm surviving. How to let Del know when I had it? How to get it to her? How to administer it had to be Del's problem.

Under what category would this information be available at the public library?

Could I consult my Ob-Gyn?

Should I forget the whole enterprise?

Too late. I had mentally passed the point of no return.

I had to go through with it.

# XX

The unfunny fun began. Hot stuff over hot coffee. The volume on the cartoon videos raised to prevent the plotting and planning reaching the sharp ears on little pitchers. We conspirators discussed this method. Threw out that possibility. Improved each other's suggestions. Saw the fallacy lurking in too complicated procedures. In short, had a highly tense time stretching our thinking power for a solve to a kooky kinky problem. Forbidden fruit scheming. That was our ticket to escape domestic boredom. Such contrivance was fraught with taboo, danger at being discovered, many ways the whole thing could backfire. It was exciting. Wasn't sex better when it was on the qt? A reason men kept mistresses and women were tempted to fool around? We didn't stop to consider all the side issues. We simply kept our eyes on the goal, a worthy goal in our sight. For if it be folly to pursue happiness, then so be it. Vive la bagatelle!

We kept it basic. Sex with John. Condom in ziplock baggie. Delivered over the back fence to Del after I rang her phone twice and hung up. As soon after coitus as possible. Problem: John worked on his thesis most nights well into the a.m. hours. Problem counterbalance: the sperm donor fell asleep almost immediately. Except, of course, on the night of our first caper.

Our first attempt at dangerous liaison imprinted such indelible images and retentive feelings that time has dimmed them not. The exercise included near discovery, adrenalineboosted improvisation to cover an unexpected contingency, and a heart-stopping narrow escape. John and I had sex at one sixteen a.m. (digital clock, visible in the dark) I was so impatient to be done that I almost used those three little words outlawed by Dr. Ruth, 'Are you coming?' Hung in, not wishing to arouse suspicion by acting out of character.

Lying awake, waiting for someone to fall asleep in order to perform nefarious deeds, was eminently worse that watching actors waiting for Godot. Morpheus withheld his favors for a quarter of a century (of an hour) before I felt it was safe to ease out of bed. To navigate a stairway by toe and fingertip touch. To switch on the small light over the kitchen sink So far, so good. Crikey! A voice from above!

"What are you doing down there?"

"Uhhh . . . Ruff-Ruff needs out."

"Wasn't he out after dinner?"

"Yes. But I guess not for long enough."
"It's pretty late for you to be out in the yard. Do you want me to come down?"

"No, no! Don't come down! I'll be perfectly safe with Ruff-Ruff. Go back to bed. You need your sleep. No need to come down. Really! Come on Ruff-Ruff, old boy. Out we go!"

Ruff-Ruff's instructions were given with my finger hooked into his collar as he lay on the familyroom couch. Ruff-Ruff didn't like being disturbed. Said so.

"Why is the dog growling?" Called over the bannister.

"Because you are keeping me talking and he wants to go out!"

I opened the back door. It was mighty dark out there. It was a good idea to drag Ruff-Ruff out with me. He stretched and yawned and deigned to accompany me. Del did not. Of course not! I had forgotten to ring her phone two times! Nothing for it but to creep back into the kitchen, muffle the dialing beneath my robe, listen for the eternity it took for the darned thing to ring twice. Slipper-foot it across the wet grass to the fence and wait some more. I feared that the sun would come up before my partner in folly appeared. A fast, wordless transfer because Ruff-Ruff felt it his duty to woof off a couple of barks to greet Del. John's head stuck out the bedroom window.

"Are you guys almost done out there? Are you okay?"

Del had flattened herself against the wall of her house in a James Bond movement. Or commando tactics.

"Yep. We're all done. Come on Ruff."

Ruff-Ruff had found that he liked being outside in the night. He refused to return indoors. He trotted the backyard's perimeter and circled the picnic table to elude capture. Soggy scuffs were not the shoes for midnight athletics. I stopped chasing. Ruff-Ruff squatted, panted his tongue-lolling doggie smile, and allowed his mistress to pick him up. Between the dew, the wet dog, and about a gallon of nervous perspiration, I was soaked to the skin. But, by thunder, Mission Accomplished!

The indoor thunder came from John's snoring. Lucky him. He could sleep. I could not. I tried to visualize what Del might be doing. I had told her a turkey baster would work. She had insisted on buying sterile medical syringe things. It was her baby, after all. I hoped.

## XXI

Babies are supposed to be conceived somewhere slightly before the midpoint date in a twenty-eight day menstrual cycle. This study presumes that menstruation is as regular as clockwork. Some women's cycles run true to form. Some normal cycles may vary by as much as two weeks. Del and I had decided to ignore counting and temperature-taking routines for two very good reasons. I had conceived Benny about six days following the onset of a period, and Bobby, at least eighteen day ditto. This suggested a wider window of opportunity, and what we had to deal with was an irregular regularity wherein supply and demand functioned in no synchronous arrangement. In other words, John had to be in the mood. He had to be kept in the loop as an uninformed participant.

Practice did not make us perfect in deception. We did get better at it. I learned keep my eardrums taut to listen for the breathing pattern charastic to sleepers. Some nights, a struggle to keep awake, I even stooped to reciting all the nursery rhymes I could recall. Hickory dickery dock became my regular nocturnal incantation. A plea.

"Hickory, dickory, dock/Hurry up you goldarned clock!"

The clock paid no attention. It flashed its red numbers at its own pace, actually seemed to elongate the minutes during the fifteen-minute grace period I waited to be sure that John was sound asleep. Ruff-Ruff got used to a post-midnight romp in the night garden. He stopped barking at Del. I forestalled his rascal attempts to stay outside by carrying a cookie to bribe him when it was time to go indoors. He fell for the trick every time. Operations proceeded smoothly through May. Del had not skipped a period, but she and I both optimistically agreed that it was early days, yet.

June found John's thesis in a presentable state. His latenight labors ended. We went to bed earlier, at the same time. John, however, lay between the sheets reading towards organizing his bibliography. Made the crusade more difficult, but not impossible. He took longer to surrender to sleep, and his sleep ran to the restless variety. His tossing and turning promised not that he lay truly dormant.

Apparently, some nights I misjudged. He was not so sound asleep as to be impervious to sounds. One sunny morning he asked a question that nearly resulted in a mis-pour from the coffee carafe.

"Who are you calling on the telephone so late at night?"
Answer delayed by repeating the question. "Who am I calling?"

"Yes. Who are you calling? The extension phone in our bedroom clicks when we dial the downstairs phone. I picked it up last night but there was no conversation. What gives?"

A scattered wits recovery. "Oh, that call. I call the time and temperature information number."

"You need to know the time and temperature in the middle of the night?"

"I do. It . . . it helps me plan the day. You know. whether the boys and I will be able to go for a walk ..or if we should hitch a ride with Del to go to the library ..if it will be raining." Went a bit too far, there.

"They give you the weather report? I didn't know that."

Recouped. "Well, not the weather report exactly, but stuff like the ..ah..humidity."

The sports section of the Plain Dealer ran interference for me. The heat was off. Almost.
Checking baseball scores. "What is this riding to the library with that person next door? You can have our car any day you want it."

I know. But it takes so much time to drive you to work and maybe have to make a second trip if you can't get a ride home. Del doesn't mind. She did babysit free for us to go to the wedding. And she's all alone over there right now."

The newspaper took a rattling shake. "Okay. But I don't want you two becoming bosom buddies, or anything."

'Bosom buddies'? I came this close to, 'O give me a break!' but realized just in time that my husband had no idea he had uttered a double entendre, English major or not.

His telephone click discovery did indicate the necessity for a major change. The two-ring signal was out. My solution worried me because it added to Del's hardship. Del staunchly declared she didn't care. She told me she wanted to get pregnant in the worst way. I laughingly asked her what could be worse that what we were doing?

Del, serious, "Failure to overcome any and all obstacles."
We had decided upon a light signal. Our west wall faced Del's house. Two-thirds of the way up our flight of stairs, just before it right-angled on up to the second floor, there was a small, circular window. Other than a window in the boys' bedroom, it was the only opening that Del could see from her east, rear bedroom. A flashlight beam to wait for was less convenient. It meant that Del had to stay up keeping watch. Tedious, to say the least, especially on the nights when no signal happened. Del could not sit up all night, every night. If nothing was going to happen, I arranged with her to signal three short flicks of the flashlight no later than two a.m. The sun was rising earlier every morning. Benny and Bobby woke up at first light. Fatiqued unto snappish, I set my weary brain to the task of finding a less energy sapping system.

No solution occurred to me. John gave me a good news, bad news break. Home computers had not come into vogue at that time, but John had made use of the community college computer and its office copying machine. A small college near Erie Pennsylvania had liked his resumé and invited him for an interview. Held out a summer job carrot, and a deanship vacancy to be filled in the fall. To laugh, or to cry, that was the question. Whether it was nobler of the mind to wish John good luck, knowing full well what a gigantic effort was entailed in such a drastic relocation, or to indulge in a selfish selfcenteredness, and protest too against what I believed to be the sneaky way in which the job application was done. No joint discussion. I sacrificed a justifiable indignation argument and feigned a neutrality. An angry John Del and I did not need. There was always the chance he might not be hired. Another deciding factor, John would be out of town for a week. I would be able to go to bed and sleep. Del would be able to go to bed and sleep. If Del was only half as exhausted as I was, no wonder at all that she had not gotten in the family way.

John got the job. The salary and prestige entitled him to refer to it as a position. He would teach a class in English Compostion for seven weeks of the summer, familiarize himself with the college routine for another paid week, reign as head of the Arts Department for fall and winter semesters, then step into the retiring dean's shoes the following year. For the summer stint, he would be boarding near the Dunedin-Tarylton College. He would come home for weekends. For Del's sake, I had to stay on good terms with this traitor. 'Coming home for weekends' I read as a code phrase for coming home for sex. Del and I faced a decreased sperm supply, but maybe upped the quality and sperm count, this enforced abstinence. A more rested Del might conceive more readily. We held our breaths for three days in July. Del was late. Alas, a cruel false alarm.

Alarming alarms occurred during that summer, plus one marriage-threatening crisis. My sex seeker came home one weekend. He had coerced Mater and Pater Saddle to babysit. The children would be in bed, so they truly had to do nothing but sit. Their son had made reservations for dinner at a restaurant in the suburbs. It was, literally, a log cabin, complete with pioneer-type fireplaces, serving steaks hot off the old homestead grill. Frenched potatoes fried in beef fat. Ah, those days before cholesterol awareness ruined our appetites. Coconut cream pie to die for if the steak failed to clog our arteries. A courting ritual revived.

A memorable interlude ensued in our bedroom. A totally satisfying experience. Bacchus smiled on me. The wine god's ambrosia lulled my lover into a soon sleep. A slither out from under John's arm, baggie in hand, and I would have been on target if I could have found the flashlight. I rmembered that Bobby had been fascinated with it earlier in the day. Switching it on and off. Giving it the once over as to how it was held together. Lest he succeed in taking it apart, I had put it someplace safe beyond his reach. Downstairs.

I trod lightly into the hall before slipping into my robe and inserting the baggie into its pocket. Expertise comes with repetition. I could navigate the trip down the stairs blind-folded if need be. The unlit familyroom proved a bit more of a challenge. A grope lit a small lamp to lighten my darkness for pats along upper shelves, digs under tables, and delves among the couch cushions. The latter moves disturbed Ruff-Ruff, who naturally assumed it was night romp time in the garden. His bounce to the floor sent a four-stack of video tapes aclatter against the coffee table legs. Cause a pause for deep listening. No one but me seemed disturbed.

Ruff-Ruff gambolled among my ankles, inhibiting my progress in the hunt. His toenails went tick-tick-tick on the kitchen floor as we widened our search. Telling his to, "Sit!" sent forth my hissed command and his one bark reply to refuse to do so. It was all a game to him. When had his tail wags become so noisy? And his breathing so asthmatic? An eeriness crept over me. This escapade was taking too long. Some other light had to be used to send the signal. It came to me in a flash. Two candles sat on the diningroom table. I knew exactly where the matches were hidden. The wick caught and held a pinpoint flame. Ruff-Ruff squeaked his dislike of fire and smoke. Holding the candle aloft, I bent to rub his ears while I used mine. All quiet?

The candlelight danced at its own reflection in the round window's jewel-colored glass. The candlestick holder moved up down to reinforce the altered signal. A loud demand nearly shocked the whole kit and kaboodle into a fiery tailspin.

"What in blue blazes is going on? Who do you think you are? Lady MacBeth?"

Ruff-Ruff cowerd close to my bare feet. I took more trouble than necessary to calm the candle's flame.

"Well? What is going on? Vic!

Self-protectively resentful, "You've scared poor Ruff-Ruff! grasping at a straw excuse, "I wanted to check on the boys, and I couldn't find the flashlight . . . I didn't want to turn on the light in their room." Chin jut forward 'so there' posture.

Here it came. "You know, Vic, if I live to be a hundred I never in this lifetime understand you. The boys are fine. Come back to bed."

Stubborn. "As soon as I've seen for myself."

I made a show of monitoring my sleeping offspring, candlelight palm-shaded. A dissected flashlight rested beside Bobby.

John was wide awake. His body fought the mattress for a comfortable position. His twists and turns churned his digesting steak and wine into heartburn acid. He shuffled to the bathroom and called me to come find the Alka Seltzer. The labelled bottle sat front and center in the medicine cabinet. The fizz in the tablets prompted him to pace the bedroom floor and burp repeatedly. He wondered, aloud, if a few crackers might be helpful?

Crackers was a word familiar to Ruff-Ruff. He set off after his master to keep John company at the kitchen table. Head cocked at the ready to spot any falling crumb. John surfed the channels to catch a late-night movie. Clint Eastwood, wrapped in a sarape, met his gaze. John settled on the couch. Ruff-Ruff settled for the recliner. I accepted defeat. Where I lay just as wakeful, worryied to death about Del waiting at the backyard fence.

It was after breakfast before I deliverd the baggie. I feared that the little swimmers inside had lost all interest in creating new life. Del disagreed. It was worth a chance. To my abject apologies she offered reassurance that she had gone back inside when she noted the telltale impulses from the t.v. screen making phantom flickers on the familyroom's rear windows. I was not to worry. I promptly ignored my husband's rule re: we two becoming bosom buddies. I gave Del a really big hug. Surprised the heck out of both of us.

A happenstance surprise, interim to another close call sperm delivery, came within a hair's breadth of cancelling the 'til death do us part' vows. It began innocently enough. Staged in our own backyard. At our own garage-sale, cross-legged, picnic table.

# XXII

Mater Saddle meant well. She had experienced a minor exhilaration flutter at our heartfelt thanks for sitting the children to allow as an evening out. As do-gooders so often do, she extended a further favor to earn additional gratefulness on our part. A repeated gratification for herself. It was her way of being 'nice'. I really don't think that my mother-in-law ever indulged in manipulative hidden agenda. A fluke, truly, that her generosity backfired.

Semper paratus must have been her family motto, aided and abetted my money no object. She arrived one day, complete with a serious rival for the famous Fortnum hamper. For all I knew, the real thing. Ma and Pa arrived on the Saddles' heels. They toted along frisbees for their grandsons, a rawhide chewy for Ruff-Ruff, and for once, no potluck contribution to share with the other non-contributors; i.e., Mary Jane, Gordo, and Derek. Uncle Victor and Zelda were keeping the honeymoon going by cheering up travel agents, worldwide.

My uncle and new aunt could not have enjoyed more sumptuous dining than our stay-at-home group. Easily peeled oranges the size of small melons. Still-life class apples. Smoked sprats. Splits of bubbly. Mater Saddle unpacked and summed it up,

"All sorts of good things!"

Her evaluation seconded by her lord and master, "Quite a treat, eh wot?"

It was. The hamper's contents positively blew the collective minds of Derek and Gordo. As the substitute staff while Zelda was gallivanting the globe, they discussed whether or not some variations on the delicacies might not go over big on the high tea menu. They excluded everyone else from their discussion, which struck me as impolite. When in a Genoese group, one should do as the Genoese do. Talk to each other, sometimes all at once.

The tiny roasted quail failed to go over big with Benny and Bobby. Ma, whose ideal meal ideas depended upon pastas, cheeses, and marinara with ground meat, sympathized with her grandsons on their dead 'birdie' trepidation. She filled their plates with Danish ham bitties and baby sausagies. No sympathy from me for anyone who missed out on the splendid crackle of crispie bones nested in flaky pastryie. At first sight, the roasted birds reminded me of Mary Jane. One delicious nibble erased any such comparison. These birds were most agreeable.

For pudding, the Brit word for dessert, Mater Saddle opened a box of carefully packed, custard-filled, chocolate flans. I wished I had asked Derek to make the coffee. Mine did not do those delicacies justice.

Mater Saddle chose that sweetest moment to drop her bomb. Oh, that it had been a chef's bombe instead of her explosive idea. Again well-meaning, she presented us with a prepaid holiday for our nuclear family at a resort motel. To accommodate the children's short attention span where car trips were necessary, she had selected a resort not too far away. On Route 90, abutting a state park, and close enough to Lake Erie to include ponds and waterways to explore. John cut her off at the passing of the gift certificate to me. He insisted there was no way we could take a family vacation that summer. Registration week began in mid-August at his new college. He was committed to attendance at it. He needed time on campus to organize his fall classes. He planned to put our house on the market right away. He was fed up with the drive to Cleveland every weekend. Our old car couldn't take the road beating. Derek and Gordo ceased their private topic for two at his next announcement.

"We need to find a house closer to my work. Blah, Blah, Blah."

John's mother demonstrated the meaning of the word 'crestfallen'. If chagrin was not in evidence upon my face, it should have been. Derek mistook the reason behind my look. He tried for helpful. Ahhhhhh! Not helpful!

He had the colossal nerve to smile at me.

"Don't worry, Vickie. Gordo and I have been on the lookout for a house to share. Yours is in pretty good condition now, and we think it would suit us fine."

Gordo's turn to rub salt in the wound, "With just a bit more fixing up. A change here and there."

A split-second decision to split. I decided that the boys needed to be taken in to get ready for bed. All present knew better than to offer any objection to this plan. The last words I heard? An eager John opening negotiations with Derek and Gordo.

The water dampening my cheeks was not all splashed bath water. No sperm was made available that weekend. Nor the next.

Del did not blame me. She was ticked off at Les for staying away so long. She decided that we needed a break. And not at MacDonalds.

## XXIII

If Del had an ulterior motive, so what? Twinkle in her eye, she suggested what a shame it was for a perfectly good gift vacation to go to waste. I came up with negatives. She parried with plausible positives. I had no transportation to get the Aupres De Resort. She pointed out that the place was on the way to Dunedin-Tarylton. John could drop the children and me off. I would be marooned in the middle of nowhere? Not at all. Del would join us in her car the next day. No way. Life in one room with one bathroom, and two children, meant early to bed and early to rise. disrupted sleep. Diaper encounters of th odoriferous kind . . . Del would have none of it. Literally. She planned to rent a room of her own. As for her ulterior motive? She was setting the scene for reconciliation between John and me. No reproach from this quarter. Holding a grudge is hard work.

As the grudgee was finding out, John began calling nightly to ask how the children and I were doing. I told him we were going to take advantage of his mother's paid vacation. Come hell or high water, he would be home that weekend to help us pack and get settled at the Aupres De Resort. No problem! He threw in that he would bring the contract from Dunedin College so that I could see in black and white all the advantages in accepting his new position. He promised, practically on his mother's eyebrows, not to buy any house that I didn't approve. I didn't plan instant approval. I wanted breathing space to hold out for one more Christmas in our fixer upper. I had put my heart and soul into that house. The real estate agents in Tarylton were in for dealing with one tough customer.

The weather over Labor Day weekend pleased no one. It pleased itself. It poured rain. Mowing our few blades of grass was out of the question. Getting down to making up for making out in the lost time department fit in 'nicely'. A Noah's ark seclusion. Lowering skies and the rhythm of the waterfall. We made good use of naptimes and bedtimes. Saturday's predawn delivery went off like a charm. Sunday's was not so lucky.

Fall nights gave Aurora short shrift in daylight hours. Sunrise came later and later. Instead of midnight Paul Revere signals, Friday and Saturday nights being the sole opportunity for harvesting, Del waited in her yard from five a.m. until I appeared. A pre-sleep set of my mental alarm clock worked for me. With one exception. It had been a dark and stormy night, a dark that lingered to obscure the dawn's early light. I awoke with a start. The clock read six. Frantic haste rustled up more thumps and bumps than stealth and slither. John stirred. Seemed to sleep on.

Del, slipper-shod, despite mud puddles and soaked turf, otherwise dressed for warmth in jeans and jacket, waited at the fence. Her reward was two baggies. No sooner were they in her outstretched hands than we were demanded to explain what was going on. By a husband leaning out through our family room's sliding, double doors.

Practice makes, if not perfect, at least quick-witted. I called over my shoulder,

"I'm giving Del my special recipe. I forgot to give it to her last night. Les might be coming home and she wants to make her something special."

John had to see for himself. Came across the wet grass. Curious.

"Isn't Les a chef or something?"

Del dimpled, "Yes. But she really likes the—the ah-cookies that Vickie makes. The ones with all the nuts in them."

I had to complicate things with my two cents worth.

"I was letting Ruff-Ruff out and I saw Del in her yard .. so I ran in and got the recipe for her."

Unconvinced. John eyed Del.

"You were gardening this early in the morning?"

"Del blushed. Stammered, "No—no. I was—I was jogging around the yard. Not gardening. I don't feel safe on the street. Ohhh oh! I'm cooling down. See ya! Gotta get at it!"

Demonstrating in fast departure, Del sloshed off in a dogtrot around her backyard's perimeter.

I got busy brewing coffee. John brought in the paper. Still suspicious? He wouldn't let it go.

"There are more nuts around here than are in cookies. How come you've never baked those nut cookies for me? What's so special about them?"

"They're too expensive to make too often. They take lots of butter—and cashews—and imported chocolate flakes."

"Well, make some. They sound good." One more sally, "And why does that nut next door jog in her bedroom slippers?"

Whew! A toughie. "I guess its because she's moving to California, soon. Probably doesn't want to invest in highpriced athletic shoes until she sees what people are wearing out there."

John chewed that over a piece of toast. "I guess that makes a crazy kind of sense. California. Who knows what goes out there."

I refilled his coffee mug. Solicitously. Paid close attention to his final words on the subject. His hypothesis on my peccadillos had become more inclusive.

"Women! If I live to be a hundred, I swear I'll never be able to understand you women."

Maybe not, but my John had come home to unsnarl one knotty problem holding up the vacation at Aupres De. We could leave with him later that afternoon. Be dropped off for a fun time while he, poor thing, continued on to keep his professorial nose to the grindstone. And, bless him, he had seen to it that Ruff-Ruff would be taken care of. He had arranged for Mary Jane to house and dog sit.

The fait accompli was irksome. It was take it, or not leave for the vacation. I took it.

Del would join us the next day, Monday. Of course Les was not expected to come home. No need to bake cookies. All the same, Del owed me a phone call to San Francisco to get a recipe for some cashew and chocolate concoction. My head would be on the chopping block until John had those mythical cookies in his mouth. And I absolutely should learn to keep my big mouth shut.

## XXIV

A residual smattering from highschool French classes translated 'Aupres De' as meaning 'close to' or 'nearby'. Did a ninety-minute drive from home door to resort door qualify the motel as being close to Cleveland. Or a nearness to Erie, Pennsylvania? Or, More likely, a proximity to Lake Erie.

En route, later than we had planned. My fault. what wife wants a sister-in-law dog sitter to be witness to dirty dishes, a ring around a toilet bowl, dust bunnies, or a bed not freshly made up with clean sheets for the intruder's benefit? It galled to think of Mary Jane investigating our cupboards and drawers. Really rankled to imagine her offbeat friends in our house. Such speculation loaded more 'cheese' onto the down side of the seesaw antagonism. On the lighter, up side, her love of horses and animals meant excellent care for Ruff-Ruff. Despite this off-balance ambivalence towards Mary Jane's efforts, I resolved to be a good sport and not to show it. John was in a good mood, and I wanted to keep him that way. I hated it when we were on the outs with each other. Just how good a mood was he in? He made no comment when Benny and Bobby got bottles of juice, which altered them from nap-deprived cranky, to happy sleepers for the whole trip.

We took an off-ramp from Route 90, a short drive along a road below freeway level, and it brought us to Aupres De's glass and stone frontage. Vehicular vibrations ceased. The boys woke up. Potted plants made for a friendly lobby. A formal diningroom, visible to its left, was a welcome sign. We signed in. Told where to park.

The building rose two storeys high around a swimming pool, a large space, open-ceilinged all the way to the roof. The inner circle of guest rooms had rooms with a view of the pool. The outer circle rooms looked out on the parking lot and the adjacent state park. Mater Saddle had paid for the inner circle location. What else? The boys fell in love with the pool at first sight. Our room's sliding doors opened onto its tiles, lounge chairs, and umbrella tables. A four-steps-up snack bar offered fast food temptations for the swimmers. Beyond that was a barroom, Past that, one was back in the lobby.

The boys wanted to be swimmers. Immediately, if not sooner. Benny and Bobby found water irresistible. Unless it was accompanied by shampoo and washcloths. John lugged in the luggage. Suited up the boys. I preferred to squeeze into my old, prepregnancy one-piecer in the privacy of the bathroom. Better nothing said on the fit I had on the tightness of its fit. We were all prepared for a quick dip, fast hamburgers at the snack bar tables if we hurried, because John had to be on his way. He didn't want to inconvenience his landladies at his boarding house by keeping them up too late.

Broad cement steps, awash with from one-inch of water to about eighteen inches deep after the lowest step was taken, led down into the shallow end of the pool. The boys regarded the concrete steps. They balked. This body of water was away bigger than a bathtub. No amount of coaxing on my part, or mildly stern encouragement from a father who didn't want his sons to be wimps, persuaded either son to wet one toe. I sat on the first step. Made the mistake of finger-flicking water droplets in the boys' direction. They backed up to put added distance between themselves and the pool splasher. John reminded us that he did not have time for this nonsense. I achieved a compromise. He would stay with the children while their mother did a few laps to demonstrate what fun swimming was. I reminded John that we had all week. Benny and Bobby could just watch, this time. I stoked the crawl back and forth the pool length.

I had a disapproving audience. The boys wailed and screamed, "Mommy! Mommy!" They thought I was drowning? The other guests thought we parents were inflicting cruel and unusual torment on our children. We packed it in and ate hamburgers and fries with a daddy who had to leave us, but who was kind enough to care about us.

"You know, Vic, I won't be all that far away. If things get too tough, give me a call. Okay?"

Things were okay. We made progress after Daddy left, if hanging against the balcony railings outside our double doors to stare in fascination at the pool from a safe distance, could be called progress. Finally, bored with that, and assured that the pool would remain at a distance, they reverted to their more normal sibling rivalry. They struggled over which one of them would gain custody of the remote control, a gadget alien to them. At home, I could have retired them to their bedroom. Not so, in the claustrophobia-inducing, two queen-size bed arrangement. They had napped later than usual. Starchy foods, digesting to sugar, made for hyper activity. The excitement of a strange place did nothing to lessen their excess energy. As most children are, they were cunning enough to know when they could get away with murder.

I rescued the remote control before Bobby dismembered it, or found a way to use it to make the television set fly around the room to its destruction. The little devils began awkward pillow fight attempts. Thwarted by the big bolsters, the beds became trampolines. They were having a marvellous time. I experienced an insight into Ophelia's madness. The midnight hour approached before they literally fell down into a sudden sleep. Picture this. A grown woman quietly blubbering to herself, "I want to go home! I want to go ho-o-me!"

A dillar, a dollar, we were ten o'clock sleepyhead scholars the next morning. No outside window and the double door drapes had granted us an artificial nocturnal extension. We needed it. Del arrived at our room door the same time as a room service breakfast was entering aboard a shouldered tray. With Del's appearance, things began looking up. We sprawled across the beds eating bacon, cheese-creamed bagels, and strawberries. We disregarded propriety and ate with our fingers. We let the crumbs fall where they may. No Ruff-Ruff, his substitute being maid service. More fun than a picnic were the half-pint cartons with straws for Benny and Bobby to suck up the orange juice. It occurred to my funnybone that at that breakfast we were gay in every whichaway.

Del opened the drapes. Her reaction to the pool? "Wow!" Ardent advice to the contrary, she was adamant about taking two culprits swimming. She refused to take no for an answer. She sweetened her offer by asking me if wouldn't I enjoy an hour or so all to myself. I hesitated for ten seconds, then jumped at the chance. She had been warned. I had done my duty. It was on her curly head should she suffer another fiasco. A 'do not disturb' sign dangled on the doorknob. Guaranteed peace and quiet for a long soak in a hot tub, full enough to similate weightlessness. Wrapped water warmth. Rapt in a Dick Francis mystery. The chaos in the bedroom to be restored to order by maids. As an educated guess, I guessed I could get used to resort living.

Guess what. Benny and Bobby had come to terms with the water in the pool. Jealousy twinged. It was hard to admit that my sons interaction with another woman gave them more satisfaction than I did. Shades of D.H. Lawrence! Rather than rephrase the 'satisfaction' sexual overtones, I told myself to grow up! Del was their friend. Relationships between friends had to be different from relationships between parents and children. For one thing, their friends did not carry disciplinary privileges. That fact, alone, shed a whole new light on friends versus parents relationships. So much for "Sons and Lovers".

Del was great with the lights of my life. Her love of children, her patience with them, her delight in them, wasn't all that a decisive factor in our nefarious plan to get her a child of her own? Most definitely. She looked so happy sitting on the cement steps, the water lapping her waist high, Bobby going down the steps to the pool floor where the water came up to his armpits. He could be seen to take a deep breath at his own daring before he climbed up beside Del again. Benny had discovered how to hold onto the pool edge and kick his feet to make noisy splashes. They noticed their spectator mother, and gave her back her sense of importance in their lives.

"Mommy! Mommy! Look at me! Watch me, Mommy! See me swimming, Mommy?"

It was my turn to sense Del's sense of what she was missing. So deeply despairing. I felt for her down to my very bones.

Memory plays tricks. It is not infallible. It differs from short-term to long-term recall. One thing for sure, I did, do, and always will remember the affinity I felt with Del's hopes to have a child of her own. I try to remember that, because otherwise, this 'A' personality type, the type that cannot brook failure, especially in the moral standards area, has to carry a guilt forever. And a day. A lettered ancient wrote that God forgives us if we seek forgiveness. Self-forgiveness is tough to handle. Memory plays tricks. Push a button and self-condemnation keeps coming back, not like a song, but a dirge.

Thank God (reverently) our vacation had not become a memory at that time. It was ongoing and vacationers were having the time of our lives. It was my first break from routine responsibility in over four years. We ate, drank colas, and were merry at the Saddle's expense. Boon companions, we. Del introduced us to activities I would have given a miss had the boys and I been on our own. She insisted that people with the surname 'Saddle' had to try riding.

Where the resort property met the state park boundary line, a dozen for-rent horses earned their living. Some grazed in a fenced meadow behind the stable, a few gazed at us over the top of horizontally split doors. We walked the line returning their inspection of us. Del talked to them. Rubbed their noses. Patted protruding necks. Benny wanted a chance to be friendly, too. A mother has the right to feel less than confidant in such a situation, but I put up a good front for the sake of my children. Okay, so I didn't want Del to know waht a fraidy cat I was, either.

Del selected a rangy animal, long of limb and light of color in mane and tail. She said she had chosen the spotted mare because the horse reminded her of me. I stoutly denied that I had nothing in common with that horse. Insult. I did not look like a horse. I had fallen for Del's teasing. She quickly amended her remark. She didn't mean that I looked like a horse. She had chosen the spotted mare, she said, because like me, it looked dependable. Fast thinking on her part. For, in truth, Motley, the pied creature, did have a trait that reminded me of me. a tall stature. I darned well knew that I didn't look spotty. And I wasn't too happy about her saying that I looked dependable. It made me feel dowdy, matronly, over the hill.

I sulked. Motley stood steadily dependable. Del saddled her. The stable hand offered to equip the horse. Del preferred to do the job herself. Benny watched the buckling and bridling. Bobby discovered a tackle box full of intriguing odds and ends. He latched onto those with the puzzle solver's delight. He worked diligently to find any bits that fit together, and more intently to see how they came apart. He lost all interest in the horses.

Del held Benny's hand, and Motley's lead rein with her other hand. She led Motley in a walk around and around the yard. To a mother's eye, that procedure looked safe enough. Benny then waited at my side while Del emulated Chaucer's pilgrims and cantered down the lane, and urged the horse into a trot on the way back. Riding double, she and Benny sauntered hither and yon within eyeshot. Even so, it was a relief to receive him and put him down on solid ground.

The worst was not over. Del and Benny wanted me to sit on the horse. I begged off. They insisted. If Del held the bridle, I would give it a try. Once up, I looked down. I think that I realized the same emotions Sir Edmund Hillary must have experienced upon reaching Mt. Everest's Himalayan peak. I felt that I was looking at the world from the highest point on it. Motley pawed the ground. He wanted to be off. I wanted to be off. I got off so quickly that my foot stuck in the stirrup, and my behind thumped onto the muddy earth. There sat I, one leg pointing to heaven. Motley swung her thick neck around to see what was the matter with this crazy passenger. We came nostril to nose. Motley gave me the wet benefit of a snorted raspberry. The horse and I had made everyone laugh. I liked that. The horse and I had another thing in common. A sense of humor. Del was forgiven.

Benny begged for another ride. Del and he used up the rented hour. The stable owner presented Bobby with leather strap pieces that hitched and unhitched through rings and hooks not unlike the catch that attached Ruff-Ruff's leash to his collar. Pleased as punch with his sack of booty, Bobby marched along with me to the petting farm. He got to insert the quarter that released grain into a tin cup. Feeding the goats thrilled us. The little beasties kept their teeth together while they liptickled our palms to take off the corn.

Kosher or not, we invaded the pool to rid ourselves of the stable and the petting farm smells. The problem had become not how to get the children into the pool, but how to coax them out. Benny's latest feat ran to face dunking in one second submersions, each bobbing up instructing me to watch him duck under and bob up again. Bobby experimented with lying on the cement steps, try-to figure out how to do the same in the deeper water of the third step without his face going under. When their lips turned blue, time was up. They fell for the same bribery as Ruff-Ruff. Food. French fries. At the snack bar tables. Pizza, grilled cheese sandwiches, or hamburgers went with the fries. E-Coli had not reared its germy head.

The daily regimen went all to heck. No dawn cracked into our windowless room. Benny and Bobby slept later. Skipped naps, the extra physical activities, plus their mother sleeping in the same room with them, took the sting out of bedtime. The uninterrupted day allowed us to try out all the resorts pastime attractions.

The Thursday of our vacation week has remained etched forever in some stonily stubborn cerebral glitch. It was the Eve, as in

The Eve of any day preceding a signal event. The event? The roof fell in. It was Del's last day with us. We planned it to be special. We rented a flat-bottomed boat. It had shortened oars attached permanently to universal joints in its sides, forestalling the loss of them by greenhorn boaters. Bobby sat in the stern beside Del who guarded him from becoming a man overboard. Also, she was the ounce of prevention that sat sentry to the non-removeable oars. He saw a challenge in them he was loathe to refuse. Benny occupied the prow, the lunch basket packed by the Auprès De's kitchen staff at his feet. I took hold of the oars and rowed, my back to him. Circular motion strokes propelled us away from the reedy bank into more open water. Not so far out that we couldn't spot any wildlife on shore patrol for waterbugs and fish.

A great blue heron waded among the cattails, his beady black eyes and beak on the ready. This birdwatcher identified him as a heron, not the look-alike crane. He had glided down to the shallows with his neck tucked back. Cranes fly with necks stuck straight out. The heron on his stilt legs, his neck stretched to its full height, stood almost five feet tall. we paused to watch him hunt. However, the closeness to a winged monster who could look a person in the eye at eye level, who sported a beaky dagger, gave me a pause of the nervous kind. I suddenly felt a whole new respect for researchers who live among gorillas on mountains, lions on open plains, or who follow elephant herds that roam wild on African preservations. Alfred Hitchcock's 'Birds' movie no longer seemed so farfetched.

The muskrats entertained, rather than threatened. They paid us scant heed, but they kept their radar whiskers above the water surface as they swam just in case we trespassers made a false move. A Canada goose 'V' formation followed its leader to settle on the pond amid great flaps and nasal honkings. They were birds wise to the ways of tourists. Tourists meant crumbs.

We rowed on with a feathered escort in tow until we found a little jetty to tie up the boat and disembark. An area had been cleared for fun and games. The fresh air had whetted our appetites. The only voices we heard while we gobbled up ham sandwiches, corn doodles, bananas, and peanutbutter cookies, were the chirps and twitters from birds. Bread is a no-no for geese. It sets up an infection in their throats. We tossed a few corn doodles their way. They did give a few hoots at our stinginess. Sparrows hopped onto the picnic table at our departure from it. An accidental sighting that every birdwatcher hopes for was among them. A dickcissel! His black bib and pale yellow patch below it gave him away. Probably migrating through. Del laughed to see me so excited. Told me I was strictly for the birds. Got a kick out of her own cleverness.

We kicked a ball around. Tossed it. Played ball tag with it. Tired from the sprinting, we flopped onto the grass until we regained our breaths. We sat up and sing-songed nursery rhymes. Del's enthusiasm for learning them spurred us on. She floated on cloud nine to be engaged in childhood verses with the children. We competed for who could give the best Little Miss Muffet scream. The loudest horn blast for Little Boy Blue. The most pitiful meows for the Three Little Kittens lost mittens. The late afternoon air grew chilly. We rowed for 'home'.

A swim negated the need for baths or showers. A babysitter, supplied by the management upon request, dined not upon quince, and pickles and mince. That watchful owl and my pussycats ate pizza with eyes glued to cable television Mickey Mouse. Del and I were the ones who would dine in style in the formal diningroom. It was her last night and we had decided to do it up in high style. As an only child, as only children do, I had wished often for a brother or sister. Del filled that void. She had become as dear as any sibling, and without the sibling rivalry stuff. All rolled into one, across the table from me, sat a dependable friend, a fun companion, a generous soul, and a co-conspirator to spice the mix. How many blood sisters fill that bill? Studying the menu I knew that vacation had been one of the best. I had help with the children, no meals to cook, and a flop into bed following each day's pleasantly tiring jaunts minus the onus of sex pressures. Not wanted for permanent, but as a temporary freedom it was delightful, delicious, de-lovely. I wanted Del to be as happy as I was, and resolved to try harder for her sake.

We came that close to living happily ever after.

Brandied coffee at demitasse strength eased us into personal conversation. I admired Del's equestrienne skills and how adept she had been at handling the ball at our picnic games. I wished that I ran with her grace, from the hips down, instead the way I did, from the knees down, my shinbones and feet flinging about in a lateral fashion. Del admitted that she had been athletic since childhood, and despite her mini size, had royally creamed the boys in elementary school in the footraces on field days. She had a question for me.

"How come you haven't asked me the question that all my straight women friends always ask me?"

Dicken's Dumb Dora, "What question is that?"

"What Les and I do in bed together."

A waitress with a coffee refill lingered expectantly. We outwaited her, scraping up melted ice cream residue with exaggerated concentration. The delayed response time gave me a chance to skirt the issue.

"I supposed that you did whatever it took to satisy each andand to reach a climax. And it's none of my business."

It was a case-closed statement. I definitely feared to tread where nosey heterosexuals trod out of perverted curiousity. Del's gay (as in light-hearted) answer took me off guard.

"Good answer! With your permission I'll use it whenever someone asks me that stupidest of questions again. Good answer!"

The babysitter had no answer as to how the motel room's bolted pictures had managed to come off the wall. Who knew? I knew that only the male with the shortest shadow knew. I told the sitter not to worry about. An overtip sent a calmer sitter on her way. The day's grand finale to the day was a splurge on a pay-for movie. Benny and Del watched a-prop in one queen-sized bed. Bobby and I did likewise in the other. Divide and conquer paid off as my motto for peace in our moving picture watching time.

Young eyelids fluttered shut moments before Meryl Streep, as Isak Dinesen, married a baron in a thirty-second ceremony, and became the Baroness Von Blixen. I didn't notice when Del got "Out of Africa". I was the only survivor left to fade the t.v. screen to black at the movie's heart-rending ending.

# XXV

We were dead in the pool water the next morning. Benny and Bobby had begged DeeDee to swim 'aden' before she went bye-bye. Del needed no persuading. I had estimated John's arrival at no earlier than four. Friday was a work day. My reckoning failed to factor in the human equation. John had missed us, felt he was missing out on a good thing, and had given his students permission to give his afternoon counselling sessions a miss. Bobby, from his lying on his back position atop the second cement step, espied John looking down at him.

"Daddy! Daddy! Watch me!"

Daddy was watching the lot of us. Particulary Del who held Bobby's hands while he flutter-kicked. Del backed towards the steps. Deposited Benny. Acknowledged John in passing.

"Hi, Mr. Saddle. Nice to see you again."

A clever move. It left me to pick from any of a dozen non-believable explanations why our neighbor was staying at the same resort as we were. From so many reasons to choose from, my brain took a long time to choose one. John got his question in first.

"What was that person doing here?"

I gave playing dumb as a stall.

"What person?"

"Get off it. You know what person."

"Oh, you mean Del. Wasn't it nice of her to drop in on her way from the Erie airport?"

"What was she doing there? Meeting that other werido?"

Giving the interrogator his question back worked for me.

"What was she doing there?" Gave me time to put a safety on my justice-for-all hair trigger. "She was seeing Les off, if that's what you mean by 'weirdo'!"

Aimed my sights on the boys, "Show Daddy what you can do in the pool. Show him how you can go underwater, Benny."

In rapid succession the day went from water demonstrations, to the snack bar menu, the petting farm, the swings, a room service supper, cable channel surfing, and how we got ready to go to bed in the big beds. Benny, in his exciement, told his father on thing too many.

"DeeDee slept with us."

John stopped towelling his hair. It was wet and stood straight up.

"What did he say?"

I gave offhand and downplayed a whirl, "She really didn't *sleep* here. She just fell asleep while we were watching a movie. She had her own room across the hall. Completely away from ours. Lighten up."

Well, he wasn't afraid of Virginia Woolf, I guessed. He set forth a one-man rant straight from the diatribes in her play. Cut short when he realized he had a lipsquivering audience of two. He forced himself to settle for a hissed message that I hadn't heard the end of thisss-'fraternizing with those degenerate creeps'. Fighting words if ever I heard them. What was I going to say the next time someone disparaged my friend? Ah, yes.

"So what! Do you want to make something out of it?"
He did. But not at that moment. A quiet, loving quickie would have smoothed over the whole incident. Gotten us over it. Unfortunately, Benny and Bobby had picked up on the tension. Ben stayed awake and stayed awake. Bobby went to sleep in fits and starts intervals to complain that his tummy hurt. John's unresolved annyoyance with me spread to include the children. His impatience with Benny only fortified his insomnia and increased Bobby's tummy pains. He blamed me for this state of affairs. For

exposing the boys to undesirables. He really was making something out of it.

At checkout time on Saturday morning he double checked on whether Del had indeed rented a separate room. Her surname eluded him. He directed me to supply that information. The clerk looked at me expectantly. I hesitated long enough for the delay to threaten an embarrassing moment. Surrendered. "Sealman." Why did I waffle? I knew that Del had rented a room of her own. Because I had decided to take part in the game called 'making something out of it'. Two could play at that game.

Mary Jane was surprised to see us home so early. Ruff-Ruff welcomed us with body language and barks. The house had an alien feel to it. Furniture had been fractionally moved out of place. Someone had chalked tiny 'x's here and there on the walls. What game was this? Had my sister-in-law thrown a drunken party in our absence? I asked her straight out why the furniture had been moved. She made no eye contact, and acted as if the matter was of no consequence.

"Oh, that. Derek and Gordo were out a few times to take measurements and make plans for redecorating."

Imagine how I liked that! Gross invasion of personal privacy. The more hurtful because Derek had to know how much I liked the decor the way it was. He seemed to give a care about people's feelings, but did he really identify with us heteros? I wondered if outsiders subconsciously wanted the people from whom they felt estranged, to feel the way they, as outsiders, felt. Complicated, decided a disillusioned I.

Mary Jane saw discomfiture. Kept at it. Picked invisible lint off her black tee. Picked at my sore spot.

"They have some great ideas to jazz the place up. Those pillar things? They're going to paint them black to make them more dramatic. They plan to rip out the whole kitchen and do it over in an Aztec motif, and, let me see,

Enough, already. "They had no business to be in our house. You had no business letting them in."

The cat who had swallowed the canary smile, "Should I have refused them entrance, John?"

"Of course not." Establishing my insanity. "Vic, don't be crazy. They had every right to be in here. They've bought the place. Have you forgotten that? "(unspoken, 'you poor thing')"

"Nothing has been signed. This house is in both our names. Have you forgotten that, Dear?"

"Are you nuts?" (no, but I was getting there)

"I am not signing. Until a deal is on paper, it is not legal."

"Derek offered a fair price and I accepted. A deal is a deal. Don't you realize what a lucky break this is for us?"

"Lucky schmucky!"

Mary Jane was having a good time at our expense. I put a lid on it by escorting Benny and Bobby into the kitchen for lunch. Mary Jane shuddered her refusal of the peanutbutter sandwiches. I offered her no alternative. John offered to take her to the salad bar at the mall. Color me paranoid. I was under the delusion that I would be the topic of their conversation. The mad woman of Chaillot fixer upper. Dimdam mad.

Talk about your persecution complexities. At bedtime I cut off my nose to spite my face. I trashed John's conciliatory advances to have sex. A pyrrhic victory. It cost too much. It penalized an innocent victim. Del, who was depending on me to help her.

John, pissed off, "That's okay with me. I don't want anything to do with a woman who has anything to do with a weirdo, anyway."

He left me cold. He dragged our down comforter off me and trailed it behind him down the stairs to sleep on the couch. I heard Ruff-Ruff growl his contention at his master's usurpation of his self-appointed bunk. They could both live a dog's life for all I cared. For two weeks, static described the state of the union. In more ways than one.

## XXVI

The honeymoon was over. Zelda was back in her tea shoppe. Del said she understood our between a rock and a hard place condition. She offered to give the boys lunch to free me up to welcome Zelda home. Zelda pressed me into service to facilitate the lunch bunch rush. After a busy two hours we took the load of our feet to sit, eat leftover sandwiches, and talk. Uncle Victor and she had toured the British Isles, seen Paris, listened to music in Salzburg, Barged along the Volga, entrained through the Alps to northern Italy where thay visited an ancient family aunt and many distant cousins. Zelda insisted that running a tea shoppe was a snap after all that. Her complaint was faked. She had loved every minute of it, and Uncle Victor most of all.

Her bliss gave me an opening to mention that my marriage was on the rocks. I wanted to make up, I'd be darned if I was going to be the first one to cry uncle. Zelda did not see our rift as serious. She knew a way to get the love boat afloat without either of us having to say a word. Her instructions: I was to go along the mall to Victoria's Secret, buy a sexy item, and slink into it at bedtime. Doubt clouded my face. Zelda mistook it for a 'too expensive' qualm. Handed over her Visa card, and I knew I was not the only one who stooped to stretching the truth.

"No arguments. Take this and charge it on us." At my head shake. "Don't say no. You'll be doing us a favor. Victor looked all over Europe to find a gift for his little Victorina. Nothing would do. I finally told him we could get you something special when we got home. Something you really wanted. Hey, maybe I should come with you and buy a surprise for my husband, eh?"

I didn't know about that. I didn't want to know about that. I told her her suggestion bore investigation. Convinced myself there was no harm in looking. Advice accepted, the credit card not. As they say today, it didn't compute. Sexy underwear did not fit in with my idea of an uncle/niece relationship. If I bought a garment at Victoria's Secret, the purchase would remain Victorina's secret.

The store smelled delicious. Feminine frills fluttered beneath subdued lighting. The salesladies must have worked on commission, they were that attentive, yet trained to allow the customer subtle display cruising. Victorians are pictured in layered bulkiness, squeezed to death at the waist. If the Victorians had a secret at all, it must have been that despite a voluminous challenge in attire, no matter the extent of undergarments, they must have had holes in all the right places. Victoria's openly offered secrets certainly did. Holes were not me. I fell for a spaghetti-strapped simplicity cut low in the back, linked to that old black magic euphemism for sex. The negligée was black. It was meant for me.

John came home for Hallowe'en weekend. Everything was black and gold. Orange pumpkins, yellow moon, shadows black as ink. Our two little clowns, who had been granted free rein in their mother's makeup kit, played trick or treat indoors. The grandparents had come over with lollypops, lemon drops, candy bars and small toys. Our street was not conducive to night roaming and few, if any, would answer knocks on the door in daylight, let alone in the dark. I sided with John when it came to Benny and Bobby's safety. He saw this cooperation as a chink in my armorstubborn refusal to move. Our parents saw the wisdom in a move to a town-type community. If their pro comments were few, it was because they were loathe to put distance between themselves and their grandsons. They made the most out of filling witches-on-broomstick plastic bags. Avoided the writing on the wall. Kept up a party mood. The pizza man arrived in time to do his bit to keep us happy. Happy was nice. And if Victoria's black nightie could pull it off, this was to be the night of resumed conjugal bliss.

Victoria did not deserve all the credit for success in the vamp department. John was fed up with trying to get comfortable on a dog-dented couch. He needed stress relief from testerone buildup. He saw a wife showing signs of relenting on the move from our fixer upper. Timing was everything, but in all fairness to Vicoria's Secret merchandise, the spaghetti straps deserved some praise. The least shrug and they slipped right off the shoulders.

The afterglow cuddle brought to light John's confession that he knew there was nothing sexual going on between Del and me.

Laugh or cry? Give me a break! imploded his presumption. I was having sex to get the sperm to deliver in the crumpled baggie to give to the maiden all forlorn so that she might get pregnant. This was nothing sexual going on? Whether or not, Del and I were back in business. We had fixed upon a three a.m. time to give our product its best chance. Important, John was in his deepest sleep at that hour. I slipped up once in November. I fell asleep, and a later dawn caught me napping. Haste made for a rash dash. John caught up with me at the back door. A jump out of my skin got a near miss. For sure, on that occasion, John challenged my ingenuity.

"Where are you going at this hour in your robe? It's freezaing outside."

"I'm ... putting out birdseed. I forgot to fill the feeder last night. You know, what with everything to think of, the move and all, and the birds come for their breakfast the minute it starts to get light."

John stood perplexed. On a fresh intake of breath I dealt him some underhanded female flattery. Stooping to conquer.

"I wouldn't have dreamed of going outside so early unless you were home to help me if I needed it."

Seed out, we went to bed. Del had either given up or had the sense to stay in concealment. My compliment had made John feel so gallant that he helped me off with my robe. Wouldn't you know it? Those spaghetti straps just refused to stay put.

John would not stand still for any Thanksgiving observance that year. His four-day weekend was reserved for our joint trip to show me Dunedin/Tarylton College, and for a real estate agent to show us the house that John thought I might like. Feigned cooperation covered one of a multitude of sins. Veiled, but uppermost in my mind, my determination to be foot-dragging where it came to house approval. Unto the likes of the Taj Mahal. Ma and Pa volunteered to stay at our house. Mater Saddle paid for a student majoring in Education to relieve Ma each morning until

Benny and Bobby went down for their afternoon naps. Everyone had conspired to forestall my strongest argument, the one against both John and I being absent from home at the same time.

How long had it been since John and I had been child-free, and bedded overnight in a motel? Since our honeymoon. In other words, forever. John's immediate concern was house tours. He betrayed a secondary goal when he hinted that I pack that 'black lacey thing'. What a shame it was that Del's and my primary goal would be unable to receive any benefits from those three motel nights so far away from the backyard fence. Nothing for it but to submit to lovingly persuasive attention, meals ala menu, and room service. I could do that.

Not a motel, but an inn was to be our abode. John had reserved a room at the Plain Victuals Inn. (pronouced 'vitls') The Vitls Inn was two miles out of town. Cape Cod had influenced its decor. It certainly knew the value of puffed pillows piled on fourposters. Either John's mother knew about this inn, or my husband had inherited more of her genes than was usually apparent. Some entrepreneur had perfected a place to be pampered. With perfect, rather than plain, victuals. Boiled dinners may have slipped from grace, but a genuine New England dinner is to die for. We figured we could not go wrong on the house wine. Along with the boiled dinner, I got quietly stewed. Had I stayed quiet, I would not have gone wrong via loose lips in the bedroom.

The main objective got right on target, eventually. There was a lot of rolling about and tumbling around, silliness, an aftereffect brought on by the house wine. So who was counting on a scale of one to ten? Being slightly pickled made the fooling around that much more fun. I remembered a chase and a pillow fight. John remembered that he forgot the condom ritual. Before we fell asleep he apologized most soberly. The giggles still controlled me.

"It doshn't matter. I forgot the baggiesh, anyway."

"Good Gosh, Vic, we don't have to worry about the plumbing in a hotel! Good grief!"

"Sharlie Brown."
"What?"

What was I saying? What was I thinking? Instant sobering. I had been dangerously close to letting the cat out of the baggie. I took the pledge to no more drinking alcoholic beverages until Operation Del was over. Suddenly gay again—the cat out of the baggie reran as hysterically funny. I became a helpless victim to a fit of giggles as I cuddled up to my big strong lover who had gone to sleep thinking he was going to sell me on a house the next day.

# XXVII

The agent greeted us with a smile. She worked out of a storefront office on Maine Street, a placard in the window read 'Maine Street Realty'. I liked that, straigtforward and to the point. Despite that appeal, its future to sway this rebel from her chosen path looked dim. A thumbs down reception was preordained for any house up for sale.

Mrs. Heughen, salt-and-pepper hair perm frizzed above a blue blazer that matched her bluer eyes, introduced us to her blonde, ponytailed daughter who wore the loose comfort of a post-partum tunic with buttons down the bodice for nursing convenience. The new mother, Lizbet, granted us a peek into the baby-bumpered, hand-quilted crib. Petal pink and pale gold perfection if ever I saw it. A month-old girl child slept as fair as a lily, displaying her Pennsylvania Dutch heredity. An involuntary throb twinged through the area where I supposed my ovaries awaited fertilization. I sent them a message to quit that. I did not want any more children. Mind you, I wouldn't have minded hugging that bundle of sweetness close to my heart for a few minutes. I equated what I felt to only a fraction of the longing Del's yearning must have been. If I stuck to my guns, and held out on the house choice until after Christmas, we could celebrate one last Christmas in my beloved fixer upper and hopefully give Del a few more chances to have and to hold a jewel as precious as tiny Katrinka.

No problem. No Academy Award acting required. The first house stank. It oozed dampness. It reeked of basement mould. Mrs. Heughen's technique must have been to start at the bummers on her list and work up. She crossed that realtor's challenge from her clipboard.

The second house's best feature lay in its being next door to the neighborhood school. A wide lot kept it apart from the playyard. Its shrubs, trees, and evergreen plantings had been allowed to run rampant, perhaps to screen out the noise of children playing and provide some privacy. Inside, the house was still in the forties as to floor coverings, fixtures, and thick in wallpaper layers and paint coats on the enamelled woodwork. John winced at the look I flashed his way. It dared him to even think about another fixer upper in our lifetime. We declined a quartet of driveby's. Their exteriors unsatisfactory from the get-go. I had the feeling we were killing time.

Mrs. Heughen gave her wristwatch a glance. She did have an attractive listing that she seldom bothered to show. I smelled a setup. The owners refused to put an asking price on it, and, she explained winking at John, they were sort of eccentric.

They wanted to find the exactly right buyer for it, people who belonged in the house, of all things. She couldn't show it until after lunch. She would be happy to pick us up at the inn about two. That would give her time to relieve Lizbet who was working on an as-needed basis since Katrinka had been born. Lizbet needed to leave the realty office before twelve to prepare lunch for her husband and to breast feed the baby. It occurred to me that Norman Rockwell was alive and well and living in Tarylton, Pennsylvania. On second thought, would living in such a town be all that bad an environment in which to raise two sons?

A crisp green salad paved the way for our palates to revel in creamed chicken chunks over puff pastry. Dutch apple pie for afters was a reminder of the state's early settlers. For the first time in a

Benny's age, we renewed our acquaintanceship with a 'nooner'. Was that a smile on the lips of that nice little old lady, Mrs. Heughen, when she picked us up?

She drove us pleasantly past elderly oak and elm trees, until the street dead-ended at the college campus grounds. At that juncture, a Victorian beauty reigned over an extensive slope of leaf-blown lawn. From its array of fishscale shingles, to its pointy turrets, ornamented gables, millworked dormers, and spiral finials, the house stood pristine, not as if it had been built in yesteryears, but finished only yesterday. Portico columns bordered an arched gothic door, the top third of which housed a semi-circular window, upon whose glass was etched the number 23. The total effect made my fake Corinthian pillars look sick by comparison.

I felt sick. No way could we afford this house. Mrs. Heughen sensed my dismay, but being the sensible real estate she was, she gently argued that since an appointment had been made it would be discourteous not to show up, and the house was well worth our time to tour through it. She had taken the liberty to tell the owners about us. Then John got a second wink.

"But of course they know all about you, Mr. Saddle, and your position at the college, since you've been boarding with the Misses Trent." My intuition proved sound. It was a setup.

Three maiden ladies greeted us at the door before the knocker got a chance to announce us. They graciously led us from the entry hall at the foot of a stairway sporting newel posts and ascending wainscotting, into what was no scrawny parlor. Mrs. Heughen performed the introduction honors for meeting me. The three thin unto fragile triplets already knew John. They were dressed alike. Their three cottonball hairdo's knotted into three donuts at their three napes, they were alike as clones. Six unfaded blue eyes regarded us from porcelain complexions, finely lined, but only visible upon close inspection, as we toured and they talked.

Their grandfather had founded the college. Their father had been its president and had designed and built this house. They had lived in it all their lives since their births, scant minutes apart. Their mother had died when they were five years old, so they had felt it their duty to stay with their father. One had been a nurse in the original Tarylton hospital, unrecognizable now for an architectural landmark because it had sprouted wings and a clinic annex. One had taught English on campus. The third triplet had been nothing in particular—as she put it-but everything in general to manage the house and home. She had done it to perfection. We could see her skill as we investigated the various rooms. Every nook and cranny was in tiptop repair, and more importantly, had been kept true to its original form.

Our table and twelve shield-backed chairs belonged in the capacious diningroom, plus cabinets and a breakfront should we ever afford them. The no-bones-about-it kitchen kept up-to-date appliances in character by virtue of being framed in traditional mouldings and bracketted shelves. A pantry! A chopping block table. Overhead racks from which to hang pots and pans. We travelled on to an honest to goodness library. Ceiling to floor bookshelves lined its walls. It could easily double as a family room. It had room enough for a grand piano. The triplet ladies excused themselves and spryly tripped away as Mrs. Heughen prepared to lead us upstairs.

Victorians tended to large families. The second floor had five bedrooms. A major drawback drawn from my frame of reference fixer upper. Mrs. Heughen, quick on the uptake, reported there was another facitlity downstairs. Smaller than this one, and I hoped so. An imperial bathtub, rimmed in marble, had survived bathroom remodellings. One could give a cocktail party in this room. Did I love this house, or what?

I adored the house, but I didn't really know if I wanted to live in it. I had brought our fixer upper back to life and invisibe heartstrings had formed an attachment to it. I felt out of my league. Mrs. Heughen said little. She didn't need to. This house needed no selling. It sold itself. She couldn't say we hadn't warned her about our budget deficiency. She answered evasively when asked, "How much?" The Trent sisters had asked us to stay to tea—hence their bustling off to get it ready-and it was the agent's guess that they would state a figure at that time. It was with ill ease that I waited upon one of the parlor sofas, despising myself for accepting hospitality under false pretenses from those three naive darlings. I accepted my fate. At least I could enjoy the fireplace and furniture for an extra half hour.

A teacart rattled and tinkled its burdens down the hallway from the kitchen. Small tables, teapoys I discovered later, were scattered ready-to-hand among the sofas and chairs, convenient spots upon which to set Prince Albert teacups while we nibled on freshly baked bread, fruit preserves, and old-fashioned comfits. Man does not live by bread alone? A serious doubt crept in where that bread was concerned. I remembered thinking such trivia.

I had forgotten John Paul the third's background. He knew the ropes. He could turn on the charm. Ease in social situations was second nature to him. I was so proud of him as he accepted tea and said all the right things. It brought home how life's daily friction rasps off the finer sides to people who have become familiar to us. Sometimes, we see only their faults. There was my John managing gracefully, enjoying tea with three 'duchesses' as if it were an everyday occurrence. Every inch of him bespoke a dean-material professionalism. Three silvery heads nodded in rapt attention and agreement to his exposition on the necessity for liberal arts programs in college curricula. They smiled at his belief that a person was not truly educated unless his knowledge included learning from ancient civilations and had access to creative energy outlets. Such as the theater, you sly dog thought I. He took his turn being listener. Captivated them with his up-front honesty on our financial condition.

Pish and tosh. We were the buyers they had been waiting for. We would be connected to the college. John reminded them of their dear father who had been a gentleman and lover of the Arts. They wanted their house to house children, again. They had seen the rapture on my face and knew that I knew how to care for this house. A new house awaited them in Florida, all palm trees and pink stucco, right on the ocean, and filled with the airiness of white wicker furniture. They wanted a change. They wanted adventure while they were still young enough to enjoy it. I guessed seventy-odd could be considered young given the Panglossian attitude. They wanted to go on cruises and see the world first class. Expensive.

Instead of revealing an asking price, they asked us what we could afford. John had that information at his fingertips. He quoted the difference between what we had paid for our fixerupper, the amount it had sold for, and what was left after the mortgage was paid off. John stated his new salary. I suspected they were already privy to that contract. The triplets looked at each other and read each other's minds. They were prepared to carry the mortgage.

The monthly payment would be one-quarter of John's monthly income, rising as his salary rose. Several hundred dollars less if we allowed them to leave some of their antique furniture treasures on the premises, rather than selling or storing it; for instance the grand piano in the library. Yes! Many of the books? Yes, and yes again. China cabinets? Absolutely fine with me. So we didn't mind? I wondered if they were teasing us with their bright-eyed prococity. We didn't mind, either way.

I reminded them that we had two boys, one who had a talent for minor acts of furnitue deconstruction. They laughed in unison,

"We antiques are used to that!"

We didn't know what to say to that. Mrs. Heughen said it for us. We should take a day to think the purchase over. The Misses Trent did not want to exert any pressure. As if they hadn't! Not to mention her mentioning that she would not show the house to any other prospective buyers until the Monday. Before I knew it, I had transferred my affections to this seductive architecture for which we would be in debt forever. She performed the mandatory business card exchange. Faxes were a technology of the future.

We lay in bed digesting the superb Yankee Pot Roast, and discussing our options for our future. John was for buying the house. Never would we get a better deal. A funny thing about our marriage, if he was pro, I had to argue con. On this debate, however, I knew full well that I would let John win. He was the party responsible for our financial security, after all. His reasons made sense. His summary, valid. Should push come to shove, I could always teach parttime. The college operated a day nursery child care for the preschool children of the staff and students who needed this service. Derek and Gordo's mortgage loan application had been approved. We wouldn't even have to work through a bank. His parents would never let us go under, disinclined as we were to ask for money, he hoped it wouldn't come to that, but it was a safety net. Was eleven-thirty too late to call Mrs. Heughen and accept the deal?

Of course it was. No champagne, so we took the only celebratory course open to us, intercourse. Making great whoopee sober enough to remember the condom. Lovemaking so intense it left me lightheaded and giddy. In the moment of continued abandonment, I snuggled beneath the quilts bemoaning the waste of all that lovely sperm.
What John heard was, ". . . flushing all that good sperm . . ."

John mistook the lament as a compliment, thank goodness for the male ego. Fondly he kissed the tip of my nose and informed me that there was plenty more where than came from. I hoped so. Del and I were counting on it.

Remember the push-me-pull-you in the Dr. Doolittle books? I was that animal. Derek and Gordo pushed for us to move out. I pulled back on the departure, stuck at a no-progress point because of my promise to myself to give Del a best shot at success in our venture. If we moved too early in December her chances would be reduced to, at best, a half-dozen more tries at egg fertilization. My push-me-pull-you had only one direction to go. It moved sideways. I told John we should call Mrs. Heughen and make our top offer, agree to storing the antiques and books on site, at the owners' risk, and then the decision would rest in the lap of the gods, or in this instance, the triplets. No hesitation on their acceptance. Signed and notarized. We could be living in this wonder before the miracle of Christmas. But not too soon before, said the conspirator in me.

# XXVIII

The College Board freed John from his duties from the second week in December until after the New Year began, in consideration of himself being present to aid his family in the relocation process. I read the between-the-lines interfence as a flutter of influence from three iron butterflies, a.k.a. the Trent Triplets.

We recruited all the muscle we could get for free to achieve the packing and loading. John thought it would take us a week, therefore out by mid-December. I had set my sights lower, and insisted they could not be adjusted. The help was too eager. Derek showed up three days running. Gordo appeared on his half day off, not to help get us out, but to measure windows for window treatment. He aided and abetted my plan. I excused myself from china wrapping and miscellaneous boxing, to hold his tape, write lengths down, inquire about his plans, and generally get in everybody's way who was trying to hurry the evacuation. So why didn't I like this asset to feet-dragging any better?

The minute Derek appeared, Gord's behavior turned foppy. Over-exaggerated hand movements, over-emphasized speech patterns, Derek's ideas over-praised. Derek was somehow less likeable when Gordo was around. I had second thoughts about them I still can't explain. Was seeing the two men together a hitting home of their anomalous sexuality? Was I jealous because Derek's attention was focussed away from me? Was I in danger of not practising what I preached to John about bigotry? Go figure. Identical feeling niggled when Les came home to exchange Christmas ahead of

December twenty-fifth; for the week immediately the holiday was the busiest in the restaurant world. By definition, 'homophobia' is a hatred or fear of homosexuals. I neither hated nor feared Derek or Del. Seeing them with their partners aroused a queer feeling in me. 'Queer' was a poor word choice. 'Irrational', more applicable. A more accurate description of how I felt I was feeling.

These vibes did not alter my wish to help Del to the utmost. John and I were sleeping on a mattress on the floor, and Benny and Bobby were with Ma and Pa . . . it was our last night in our fixer upper. I put forth a physical union as an adventure. Told John to imagine we were shipwrecked and afloat on a mattress raft. A final fling to say goodbye to our bedroom. Maybe in the movies dog-tired men revive to be in the mood. John proved a hard man to get in that condition.

"No offence, Vic, but are you becoming a nymphomaniac or something?"

He relented after his shower. "Okay. I'm a shipwrecked sailor on desert matress island. So?"

"And you haven't seen a woman for a year."

"That oughta do it. But this sailor has suffered hardships and is in a weakened condition."

"So the woman will comfort him with massage and cover him with kisses."

Del got her last chance delivery just as the night sky thinned its inky black to black pearl grey. John had crashed into a dead sleep, had his sleep out. The curtainless bedroom window let in a dawning message that it was time to wake up. His wife was missing and he wondered why. He checked out the downstairs and caught up with her in the backyard. What could I do but wing it?

With a surface nonchalance, "Oh, hi Honey. You're up early." Think/think/think/think/think!

"Don't tell me you're putting out birdseed. There's seed in it. What gives?"

Ah! A clue! "I know. But I like to put out some warm seed on these cold mornings. The birds are outside all night, you know." Tacked into the chill wind, "And how is my sailor this morning?"

Grumpily confused, "He needs a cup of coffee."

"Aye, aye, Sir! Right away Sir!" A shadow of a smile responded to that obedience.

Ambivalence prevailed as the cleaning and packing up dregs progressed. Uncle Victor dropped in to see how things were going. Ma came, minus the children. She attacked the stovie and the fridgie to leave them spotless. John, working cheek by jowl with Uncle Victor, grumbled about did my uncle know that his niece put out birdseed before the sun came up so the birds could have warm seed in the feeder. Uncle Victor did not see the joke, bless him. He always took my part. Proudly.

"You gotta remember Victorina is a trained nurtritionist. Birdseed is grain. Grain is cereal. Hot cereal is a good breakfast."

John's rolled eyes diagnosed the whole family as being rife with insanity.

When John and Uncle Victor closed the tailgate doors of the U-Haul trailer containing our last bits and pieces, I collapsed onto the stairs. Exhausted, and a bit dizzy, I accepted the glass of water Ma handed to me.

Scolded, "You shouldn't be doing so much bending and lifting in your condition."

"Yeah. I am more upset about leaving this place than I thought."

"Who are you kidding? I mean when you are in the family way."

Whole-hearted denial. "Ma! I haven't missed a—you know."

"Missed, or not missed. Do you think I don't know from pregnant?"

I admitted the impossibility because we used a you-know. While that silenced her for the moment I took advantage to ask her why I was an only child. A good Catholic would not be using a you-know?

"None of your business!"

John drove off with the moving van dragging its tail behind him. Uncle Victor came back inside. He looked from one to the other of us. Twice.

"What is going on here?"

His sister and niece in duet. "None of your business!"

Uncle Victor laughed. "Women! Get up. My woman is waiting to give us lunch."

Zelda's special lunch awaited us at the tearoom. She offered to put the boys and me up for the night. I told her thanks, but I had made arrangements to stay with a friend. With Del, actually, but no one needed to know that. Pa brought Benny and Bobby to the mall. We strolled it and browsed the bookstore, to fill in time until Del arrived to pick us up. We bought a Dr. Seuss story for the fun of imagining what green eggs and ham might taste like, and Sendak's 'Where the Wild Things Are' for the fun of scary beasts while Mom was present to protect you.

Del and I sat up well into the a.m. hours. She and Les had decided that she should list their house with a realtor. They planned to live in California. Gay couples were not con sidered as pariahs, or much more off-beat than the people who lived there. Or so Del thought from what Les had told her. She had no address to give me. When they got settled, she would mail it. I gave her our new address, 23 Trent Way. We saved discussion on our project's failure until the last minute before we retired. Tears rimmed my eyes. Del was made of sterner stuff. Played it tough with a fisticuff to my shoulder.

"Hey! You gave it your best shot. I gave it my best shot! And this past couple of weeks I think John gave it his best shot, too!"

That was Del all over. Always leave 'em laughing. Cheerful goodbyes disguised our heartsore parting to spare the boys. We waited for John to pick us up. The boys shouted to hear voiced echoes in our empty fixer upper. As we drove off, I swear it looked sad to see us go.

## XXIX

The Victorian lovely we moved into welcomed us, welcomed us warmly with a holly wreath on the front door and freshly baked apple pies in the kitchen. What an exciting time the boys had exploring all its nooks and crannies! So much for trauma brought on by relocation. Their father, John Paul Saddle, soon to be Dr. John Paul Saddle, was becoming a big man on campus and popular with the students. He had found his niche. Who could ask for anything more? He headed up the Arts Department, particularly the Drama Society; Directorship was his forte, and his work became his play. Which is what every adult's work should be.

The place had a lot going for it. So why wasn't I going full out for it? Campus pathways next door to us beckoned for walkers. Ancient trees pleased a squirrel mob, and as the bunch ran up and down the ladders on the feeders they were fun acrobats to watch. The college did have an attractive and wellrun nursery/day care center. A real plus, because I, who did not want another baby, was going to have another baby. Let me clarify that. Before this baby was conceived I did not want another baby. Once it was a done deed, of course I wanted it. I secretly wanted it to be a girl. I carried my unborn with a tender guilt. There I was, pregnant without any real effort, and Del, who had tried so undauntedly, remained barren. It simply was not fair. As it didn't seem fair to have to turn, what seemed to be a vast project, this house into home sweet home. Stuff like that took lots of time.

Faster than a speeding bullet fairly measured how fast Christmas gained in momentum towards its annual arrival that year. Cast as superwoman, I was failing in the role. We'd barely had the time, let alone the energy, to condition our psyches and position our furniture to its best advantage among the antiques before our extended families, Ma as spokesperson via long distance call, notified us that everyone had voted to spend Christmas Eve and Day with us. More pronounced than ever the depression that we had bitten off more than we could financially chew, that we had hardly paid off the mountainous bills from Christmas past, only to sucked down into the hole for Christmas present. John and I discussed the gift-giving crisis. We did what we did every year. We vowed to economize. He, sternly. Myself, wearily. All I yearned to do was sleep. The pregnancy? The state of mind? Or both?

Benny and Bobby still believed in Christmas magic. Presents for them were a must. The adults could cope with a miss, surely. On the non-coping side, our folks were trying to hang onto us. They needed to be able to visualize us in our new surroundings. We had to manage an old-fashioned Victorian Christmas and keep it cheap. For starters, no wardrobe expenditure. Clothing felt tight at the waistline, but no tummy bulge yet, so last year's sweater could stretch to the occasion. Holiday food for a dozen people would unbalance the bank account, but Uncle Victor's gift was usually a generous check. Cooking the food? Just thinking about the smell of it brought on nausea. The scene was set for a minor nervous breakdown. I began to think that Del was lucky not to be in this condition.

One lucky break. The college did not put on a Christmas season play. Its main drama occurred in the spring during 'March Merriment'. Unlike the community college, most of the students here came from faraway places and neighboring states. They did not need to live at home to get a cost-effective education. John remained free to give his lethargic wife assistance. Which he did, wonderfully well. He blamed himself for the accidental pregnancy. I share with him my theory that it took two to tango. The other part of my theory, kept to myself, was that maybe it was payback time for the way I had developed our sex life into a triple-time fandango. John called me his good sport and ran a wire clothesline contraption for Ruff-Ruff to spare me having to walk him. The yard was hedged, but not fenced. He took over the care and supervision of our two sons, singlehandedly and, important to me, patiently. They were three guys together.

Shopping solo should have been a snap. I was in control pushing my cart past the packaged and bottled grocery shelves. Patrolling the open cooler meat displays, despite styrofoam trays and plastic shrink wraps, the sight and smell of raw blood and fowl corpses did me in. I was about to lose it. Abandonned the cart. Made a mad dash for the store entrance. Met Lizbet, Katrinka cradled next to her bosom in a canvas sling, on her way in. She recognized my distress signals. she got me to the john on time. Supermarkets do not have public restrooms. They do have a closet-size necessary for their staffs. The one I barged into had one throne and a sink joined to the wall by a 'U'-shaped pipe that branched off at right angles into the wall. Spartan. It was the most appreciated facility I had ever been in. The Old Mill Road Inn's elegance included.

Lizbet did more than commiserate. Her similar symptoms had plagued her throughout her entire pregnancy. Once I had upchucked, I always felt better. I wiped my face with a wet paper towel, telling the face in the streaky mirror, "Del, being knocked up is not all it's cracked up to be."

"I thought your name was Vickie."

"It is. I'm just a little confused today."

Lizbet planted a kiss on little Katrinka's downy head. Consoled me with how even the labor pains were worth it. I knew Del would have suffered all the tortures of Hell to have what Lizbet had. Lizbet also had an idea. She explained how a girl she went to highschool with ran a catering business, and how she, Lizbet, helped Helga by baking Pennsylvania Dutch dishes which were very popular thereabouts at club buffets, local restaurants, and wedding receptions. Lizbet could prepare our Christmas dinner and I would be spared inhaling all the cooking odors. I thanked her. I told her we couldn't afford it. Lizbet was having none of that. The charges could be kept to a minimun. The meat, from cheaper cuts, say beef chuck. I argued the unlikelihood of an Italian family on one side, and veddy veddy British in-laws on the other side, be thrilled by anything less than roast goose or pasta laced with cheese and tomato sauce. She refuted the premise, convincingly to boot. When in Rome—when in Pennsylvania—do as the Dutch do: enjoy the regional cookery. One of the most famous cuisines in America. Besides, she hesitated a moment, besides, she wanted to do it on condition of a favor for a favor. Mein Gott, be that regional for Dear Lord, she had used the word 'favor'. Twice! She already had a baby so I deemed it safe to ask, "What?"

She wanted me to invite her mother to Christmas dinner. To be with a family and children instead of with other senior cit izens. Lizbet's Poppy had died a couple of years ago. Mrs. Heughen had sold their small farm, studied for her real estate broker's licence, and bought building on Main Street, Where she lived upstairs, and set up selling properties in her first-floor office. Lizbet's husband came from Vermont. It was his family's turn to have them for the holidays. Andy's mother was confined to a wheelchair and pretty much housebound. His father no longer drove on the freeway. They hadn't seen Katrinka yet.

Brother! Thought I, all this explanation was getting to be as binding as the preamble to the Constitution. There was more. She hated to leave Mooty at Christmas. Her mother was an independent soul who wouldn't butt in on other people's festivities in case she was invited out of pity, but maybe I could invite her out of gratitude for the great deal she had negotiated for us on the house. Aha! Lizbet's mother had done us a favor, we could do her a favor, allowing Lizbet to do me a favor by whomping up a Dutch-style dinner. We were into chain reaction favors? It was too much. A favor asked, a favor granted. This same altruism that had put me on the razor's edge? Inviting a lonely woman to Christmas dinner seemed harmless enough. Beneficial, in fact, because it saved me from the superstitious gloom of seat thirteen to the table, one dead within the year. A tad wary on the favor bit a second time around, I agreed to ask Mrs. Heughen if Lizbet told me what the meal would include. I had to please a mixed bag of dietary fusspots. John was a meat and potato man. Ma and Pa were pasta people. Connoiseurs, Mater and Pater. Benny and Bobby bewared casseroles as mystery mixtures of the alien kind.

Lizbet told me not to worry. What she had in mind could be served as separate items. She obliged by rattling off the menu in a whole other language. Double Dutch to my ears.

"Dutch tomato side salad, Boova Shenkel for the main course, mashed potatoes as a familiar vegetable for the children, Grishdag Ringel for dessert, fresh fruit mit kase, and lebkuchen of course, it being Christmas."

"Lebkuchen, of course?" echoed I, seeking a solve for the reason to have to have lebkuchen.

Lizbet accepted that as a declarative statement, evident by her next suggestion.

"Spumoni with them would be by your mother liked, Ja?"

I had to admit that my parents liked spumoni. What's not to like about spumoni for the people who invented it? All that candied fruit and pistachio nuts layered in ice cream. I guessed spumoni would go well with anything, including lebkuchen, whatever that was. How to find out whatever everything was without hurting Lizbet's feelings or displaying absolute ignorance? And me a nutritionist. Not so dumb. I said everything sounded delicious, and could I please have the recipes? Lizbet was pleased to so do. Alas, they would not arrive until the food was delivered on the twenty third. Early morning, as she, Andy, and Katrinka had to be off to Bennington in time for a Christmas Eve arrival at Katrinka's grandparents' house.

The food arrived as scheduled. It arrived in covered cooking pots, Saran-sealed serving bowls, lidded cookie jars, and confectioner-type closed boxes. The lot packed securely in tissue paper padding inside two cardboard cartons. Lizbet hadn't been kidding when she said 'early'. Four a.m. rated as early awakening for sure. Andy toted the carry-in meal into the kitchen in two trips, apologizing to robe-clad me in roundabout way by saying he wanted to get a headstart on the incoming weather. I waved the envelope he had handed me in farewell from the front doorstep. Dark, yes. Chilly, yes. No snow to speak of had whitened our landscape to date. I saw no reason to warn our guests who would be driving to arrive late on the morrow-Christmas Eve already! The envelope marked 'recipes' I stuck into my robe pocket. The heavy kettle labelled 'meat' went into the refrigerator squeezy-wise. All the rest and sundry spread along the pantry's wonderfully cool shelves. I went back to bed.

Who would deny a few snowflakes the right to dance in gentle spirals towards a world waiting for Christmas? A world yet clad in autumn's defoliated bleakness. Weren't we all supposed to dream of a white Christmas? The 'all' probably excluding those who had to travel for miles through blinding snowstorms. To ensure that our travellers had rooms at the inn, I had made reservations at a ma and pa, fifties vintage motel just off route 90, on the road that led to a road that led to a street that came to the turnoff to Trent Way. Plain Victuals had no room at the inn. The place had been booked for a year ahead. The motel rooms, if dated, were spotless. We could have four in a row, each had a door opening onto the parking lot, a common arrangement in the first motels. It had its advantages. No long halls to haul heavy luggage through. One's car was in plain view through what was called a picture window. The owners on site.

The folks who owned the 'Dew Drop Inn' motel had no inkling then that they were soon to trade it rich enough to condo it in Florida, courtesy of a mega conglomerate that would buy them out for the prime land location, and 'doze the Dew Drop Inn to the ground to make way for holiday inn seekers. The price was still right. Each of our guests was picking up his own tab.

The college, besides realizing the importance of the Liberal Arts in a well-rounded education, clung to its rapidly disappearing rurality by keeping a Professor of Agriculture on its staff. Dr. Mainyard's farming and animal husbandry subjects he had modernized to include Ecology concerns. The latter supported a dozen acres for farm-related experimentation and reforestation techniques. Dr. Mainyard, as he had habitually done for the Trent triplets, had tagged a tree for us to trim.

I watched my 'men' stuff their woolly hats, knotted scarves, Frankenstein boots and body-insulating stuff into our car. They were off to chop down the Scotch pine, which tree genus, claimed

Dr. Mainyard, did not shed its needles as readily as the spruce tree. The little group raised a Grandma Moses nostalgia lump in my throat. The mind, so set, engendered a need to talk to Del. Alone in the house for the first time in a fortnight, I felt the lack of her company. Once again, the telephone operator cut in to say that her number had been disconnected. I felt disconnected. At odds with my new environment. To combat the lassitude produced by failure, I attacked the diningroom table. Setting it would keep me busy and to get a headstart on Christmas Day's dinner.

The dinner! A peek at Lizbet's recipes and provisions set me in motion to check out the ingredients and the reheating instructions. The beef chuck roast, slowly steamed to tenderness, needed only warming—the better to hold its texture for carving. The breadcrumb thickened gravy, on the other hand, should be served piping hot. Dough circles, jelly-rolled around thin slices of boiled onion and potato ovals, edges pressed tightly together, were precooked and to serve warm on the same platter with the meat. Boova Shenkel, Translated, the stuffed pastalike pipelets, meant 'boys' legs'. Fun to share that with Benny and Bobby. Grischdag Ringel was a baked concoction filled with nuts, dates, and sherry, in the shape of a Christmas wreath, the wreath garnished with maraschino cherries, candied orange peel, citron, and sprinkled powdered sugar. Whipped cream optional. Lebkuchen were honey cakes, traditionally known as Bethlehem cookies. The mashed potatoes to please the children were actually little potato pancakes, their fluffiness easily revived in an oven's warmth. As for the fruit mit kase, the kase was cheese, Gouda, its red rindy roundness surrounded by purple grapes on cheese board. Spumoni had been unavailable. Neapolitan ice cream was. It was an acceptable substitute. Not spumoni, but it bore an Italian name and would go well with the lebkuchen and the dessert Ringen. Uncle Victor always solved the beverage problem. Wine. None for this pregnant woman. Fetal Alcohol Syndrome had entered the obstetric vocabulary.

My set table looked good. The weather looked bad. And worsening. At two o'clock the sun suddenly turned off its milky light and took an early retirement behind dense cloud blankets. Deceptive in their virginal white, the first earthbound floaters gave scant warning that they preceded wind-driven pellets as hard as ice. Within the hour, a plowshare's metallic rasp heralded the first scraping blitzes against the blizzard. I stood at the parlor window peering out as through a gauze bandage dimly. Concern for John and our sons, as well as worry about our familes en route in this storm, quickly trivialized the background badgering of Del's distress to a backburner. Most fervently burned my hope that Bob Mainyard had invited John and the boys into the barn to meet the horse, cow, sheep, and the goat that were a hands-on program for the students in the elective study. Followed by hospitality in his bachelor farmhouse. Drinking hot chocolate. Safely sheltered. Waiting out the worst part of the storm. How long might that take?

The t.v. stations broke into the regular programs with weather updates and reports on traffic conditions. The meteorologist pointed out blinding whiteouts on state highways. Hazardous driving conditions warnings in effect until midnight. Road crews were on the job overtime in efforts to keep route 90 open for travellers heading home for Christmas. Or, agonized I, to visit a daughter who had been foolish enough to move so far away from home. I had to do something.

Dr. Robert Mainyard's number was in the staff directory. His answer did nothing to allay my fear. My trio had left his house about thirty minutes ago. Under normal conditions they should have pulled into our driveway ten minutes ago. I dialed the Dew Drop Inn. The Ma half of the ma-and-pa proprietorship told me that the local police had asked the state patrolmen to keep an eye out for a group of cars leaving the freeway at the exit for their motel. One of the troopers on duty was a son of Dew Drop. He would see that my folks got to the motel all in one piece, and the trooper's mother would call me as soon as they pulled into the parking spaces being kept clear for them. I was finding out that living in a smaller community meant that one resident's business was every resident's business. Irksome, to a city girl. On the other hand, one's problems became everyone's problems. Like the helping hands helping out during an unexpected predicament. Like our car with John at the wheel tooling home behind a path-clearing snowplow. The driver was a second cousin to Miz Heughen. He knew that she was coming over to our house for christmas dinner, and if John parked his car just over onto the campus edge, he would see that the cul-de-sac and our driveway was plowed early in the morning so his relative would have no trouble finding a safe spot to park her car. John repeated this conversation with surprise. Right after Bobby, Benny, and he staggered in from the cold as one body.

Dried off, the Scotch pine stood at attention in the livingroom's bay window, awaiting decoration in honor of the yule occasion. Two post-bathtub, rosy cherubs in footed pajamas, waited while John strung lights through the branches. Tinsel on the ready. The wait proved too long for two young men at the end of a no-nap, exciting day. I suggested that John finish hooking on the ornaments and leave the tinsel for the boys to toss on in the morning. Hot chocolate steamed in mugs when John came back downstairs. It wasn't all that late. The early darkness made it seem later than it was. Eight p.m. was not a late hour.

I didn't like the word 'late'. 'Late' was an obituary word. The telephone rang as I raced to the downstairs bathroom to throw up the hot chocolate no sooner than it had trickled down. John kept Uncle Victor on the line. He agreed the snow had made it tough going, but for the final twenty miles they had travelled with a police escort. Sandwiches and coffee greeted them at the motel. They would all stay put until morning. Ma got on. Told me if I was doing too much to stop doing it. John said hello to his mater and pater. His goodbye included, "See you in the morning. Merry Christmas!"

The wind had ceased its eerie whistles and flutings through the millwork interstices bordering the gables, dormers, and eaves. No wonder Victorian literature abounded in ghost stories. The falling snow gentled onto the landscape. In the truly silent night, we quietly went about our sorting and tree trimming and present spreading business. Arms around each other, John and I climbed the wooden hill to bed, and therein, minded our own business. The one thrill missing was the midnight dash outside to a backyard fence. To Dell I murmured, "Merry Christmas whereever you are." John spooned himself to fit with me. Yawned, "Merry Christmas to you, too."

# XXX

Once upon a time there was a fairy tale Christmas. It took place in a wedding cake house with lacey wood trimmings, a tower fit for a Rapunzel princess, and set into a landscape held under the enchantment of marshmallow snow. Each of its chimneys descended to a fireplace hearth large enough to admit a plump midnight visitor dressed in a furry red suit. Stockings hung from the mantel shelf, their open tops hungry to be filled. Multi presents kept their secrets under wraps beneath a sentinel tree. Yes, Virginia, the Santa Claus myth lived here, holding its breath until morning.

Yea verily, a tad longer. We indulged in juice and a few lebkuchen until our family and friends arrived. Organized chaos began. People got hug squeezes. Paper tore. Children shouted to be heard. Cameras clicked. Ruff-Ruff barked and wagged. The therapeutic merry commotion brought our elderly house to life. In its element, for hadn't it been built to withstand the onslaught of big families? Oak and marble could take it. Hallways welcomed pounding feet. Bannisters held up under slides. In the mix, thanks to Derek and Gordo, coffee burbled, pancakes flipped and plates clinked.

The ohhs, ahhs, gasps and thankyou's dwindled. New toy excitement kept Benny and Bobby too busy to eat. The grownups gathered around the kitchen table for refreshment sweetened by real maple syrup, and to catch up on the news. Courtesy of Ma, everyone already knew that a new baby was on the way for us. The top prize for Surprise! Surprise! went to Mary Jane. Her thin frame had thickened unnoticeably, maternity cleverly concealed beneath a designer jacket. She was carrying twins. Trust her to do a one-upmanship! A malicious introspection on my part included, to my shame, the word 'bitch'. No one mentioned a husband or father. No one seemed upset at this omission. Mater Saddle, true to her 'good' philosophy looked 'nice' and happy about the coming event. Later, while the house tour was on, she helped load the dishwasher, and let slip a small resentment I never had suspected she harbored. Stepped out of character.

"Isn't it 'splendid'? These babies will be all mine to spoil!"

That hit home. Ma did hog the boys as if they were grandchildren that were hers alone.

The new home inspection met with everyone's approval. Derek spent an hour in the attic where the studs, et al, showed the craftsmanship of the turn-of-the-century builders. Gordo recognized the teapoys for what they were. The triplets had made a gift of them for Christmas. Gordo opined that we could send our kids to college on what the teapoys would go for at auction. He went into his exaggerated conversational mode. Flicked his wrist at what he could do with 'those windows'. How the library practically screamed for track lighting. What a creative challenge to trompe l'oeil the small bedrooms to roomier dimensions. Gordo got on my nerves when he did what I supposed was reverting to type. For that was the way homosexual males were portrayed, and I suspected they had two sets of behavior. Del was different when Les was around. Well, other than my subliminal intolerance at Gordo's criticisms, and Mary Jane stealing the limelight, the day was right out of Mary Poppins-practically perfect in every way.

A phenomenon that milestones pass unnoticed as such while they are happening. No signpost points out change on the verge. It never dawned on me that Christmas that family visits between Pennsylvania and Ohio would occur between longer intervals. I had read somewhere that if one moved twenty miles from where one has been living ties are severed. It means new neighbors, loss of close friendships, a need to find another dentist, pediatrician, and obstetrician. Patronize unfamiliar shopping areas. In short, even so short a move as twenty miles, changed one's entire life. We had moved about a hundred miles east. Telephone calls charged long distance rates. Weekly visits were out.

Aging parents preferred home to long drives. Household composition fluctuated; the future advent of twins, for example. And how had Mary Jane been so lucky, or unlucky, depending on how one looked at it, to conceive, and twins at that? A one-night stand with a fellow AA member who had fallen off the wagon and been too drunk to remember his condom? That slur brought me up short. Reminded me that a little too much wine probably had been the reason for my pregnancy. The pot calling the kettle black. For all I knew, Mary Jane might sober up and make the Mother of the Year headlines. Hey, before I had children I felt capable enough to advise anyone on how to raise the little dears. Knew up with which I would not put. After giving birth, I knew that I knew practically zilch on the subject of child raising. Some days, change that to most days, the children seemed to be educating me. What kind of hit-or-miss natural order prevailed that bestowed offspring on ignoramuses, myself included, and withheld them from potentially great mothers? I would have felt a whole lot better if I had stuck around to sympathize with Del. Fat chance. The new obstetrician had prescribed no long car trips. Bummer.

Gordo won a popularity reprieve when he interrupted a converastion between Derek and myself on the subject of finding out where Del had gone and how to get in touch with her. He claimed or proclaimed, himself a whizz at detective work. If he found Del's whereabouts I would forgive him forever for every time he pointed all five fingers at me to overstate his case.

"VIC, you DO know that FINDING your friend will be MY TOP PRIORITY!"

EAT your HEART out Old Mill Road Inn. Lizbet's Pennsylvania Dutch Christmas dinner won rave reviews. Derek sliced the roast, then warmed it. His trick to produce uniform slices. The bread was to live for. That they were devouring 'boy's legs' gave everyone a chuckle. Uncle Victor had teased Benny and Bobby, asked them if these legs were their legs. Bobby stuck his legs out from beneath his highchair to prove they were not his legs. Mrs. Heughen's face glowed with pleasure at the praise given her daughter's cookery. Winked at me.

"She learned it from her mutter, you know!"

Stuffed to the gills, we rich fish sought inertia. We migrated to the library's leather couch and armchairs. Gordo sashayed across the carpet to sit at the grand piano. A soft Christmas carol medley encouraged our laid-back mood. Changed his pedal. Added tinkles and ripples. Commanded us to sing. Derek seconded the order. Started us off with an arm-waving a-one-anna-two Lawrenc Welk downbeat.

Group singing deserves to be a revived art. The boys didn't know the words so they made noises and clapped in time to the music. Gordo swung into show tunes. A fallacy, or not a fallacy, that gays liked show tunes? I loved them. Gordo received a second star to his credit in my books. The senior guests were next to be favored with old timey songs. They belted out "Daisy, Daisy, give me your answer do", "Down by the old mill stream", "Put on your old grey bonnet!", Bye bye blackbird", "Don't sit under the apple tree", Up a lazy river". If some of us singers failed to know all the lyrics, Uncle Victor did not. He filled in the gaps and kept us going. The songfest ended with "Goodnight Sweetheart". A hint, if ever I heard one. Uncle Victor had pulled Zelda to her feet, danced her once around the library, and waltzed her into the front foyer. A general consensus ensued. An early start, on what Mater Saddle called Boxing Day, might get them back to Cleveland before another lake-effect snowstorm hit. A hubbub hustle and bustle, and then of guests there were none. People who were important parts of us who would play smaller and smaller parts in our new life.

All unsuspecting of this, John and I were not sad after the boys were all nestled and we sat close together in our Victorian parlor enjoying each other's company in the glow from the tree lights. The sweet feeling swept over me that Del and Les were together feeling the same way. Another realization popped up to increase my happiness. Christmas dinner had stayed down. Big whoop! The whoops were over. As soon as this baby was born I vowed to return to our old neighborhood and pick up Del's trail. Providing that Gordo the Gumshoe had not run her to earth by then. It WAS possible!

# XXXI

Working without benefit of a diary added to the difficulty of retrieving the details from past daily living. I do remember that I was, in a resigned sort of way, happy. Small-town living proved to be quite satisfactory. Pre-marriage, it might not have sufficed. Post-marriage, with a family to raise, it met nearly all our needs, the one exception to the positives was the geography it put between us and our extended family. We joined a nondenominational church, more for the image it projected befitting John's position at the college than for any religious aspect embodied therein. We found to our surprise that family activities; such as, pot luck dinners, programs for the children's choir, a monthly ladies' luncheon, babysitting free in the church nursery, all contributed to friendships and a fitting-in comfortableness. The college readily accepted us into its social enclave, gave us opportunities to hobnob with intelligent, well-read, and witty adults. We led a model life. Suitable, as Jimmy Cagney might have said, for the kind of hairpin I was.

This dean's wife, prosaic to the core on the outside, yet nursed an urge to indulge in some extracurricular mischief on the inside. Between acceptable busy-nesses, I missed Del. A lot. She was the sister I never had. A soulmate who made me laugh. Despite the two teenagers who lived next door who ever were eager to earn pocket money as sitters, they were not the sitter of Benny and Bobby's choice. She had spoiled them for all other sitters. Been a sitter extraordinaire. Good old Gordon had checked with as many likely real estate companies as he could. The house next door had sold for a riDICulously low amount, as he put it, and having cornered the new owners on the sidewalk one day, his one bit of pertinent information of any use was that the woman thought the previous owner had moved to California.

I gave that a few shots with calls to Los Angeles, San Diego, San Francisco, Santa Barbara and Long Beach telephone operators. Information in those cities had no listing for a D. Sealman. Leslie's surname eluded me. I have to admit that I excused myself for not trying harder on the grounds of appointments with a new pediatrician, ditto finding a new dentist, obstetrician visits a must every four weeks, a larger house to keep, my men to care for, and as the tummy protruded my body yearned for lots of naps. I had told Del my new address, but I had been a bit slow off the mark mailing it to her. Maybe she had forgotten it, or hadn't received it, and if she did have it, obviously she did not want communication between us. That was hard to believe.

I believe Mary Jane's twins arrived in June. Two girls. Maybe girl babies births were in the majority, optimistically hopeful prayed I. I delivered in August. The gods did not. My baby was another boy. When he was placed in my arms I couln't imagine that I had wanted him to be a her. While Benjamin Alister had rolled off my tongue as a name for a solid citizen, and had appeased the unexpected rebellious spark in an otherwise staid person who had nixed a 'John Paul the fourth' in favor of it, a plebian adaptation of this baby's name was to be avoided at all costs. Although the Saddles had graciously accepted their grandsons' names, I later regretted my stand against social precedent. Their jubilation knew no bounds at the names Mary Jane had bestowed upon her twin girls. Philippa, after her mother, and Paula, after John Paul Saddle the third. The name choice underwent a considerable scrutiny in the selection process on this, the third time around. I dared not name him after my father since Mr. Saddle had been so denied. Seeking neutrality, I named our baby, with John's consent,

Ma, Pa, Uncle Victor, Zelda, Derek and Gordo descended bearing christening gifts. The twins kept their grandparents conspicuously absent. Greek, or not, beware of any descenders bearing gifts. Following the baptismal water sprinkle Ma took possession of Raymond Bernard from the arms of his godmother, Zelda. Explained, as she reswaddled his blanket, that Little Ray should be taken home at once from this chilly church. A child who carried the genetic potential to exceed a basketball star's height forever would answer to the nickname 'Little Ray'. Poetic justice, and it served me right.

Little Ray, at six months of age, weighed twenty pounds, had cut his two front bottom teeth, and definitely needed to be weaned. He thrived on strained, mashed, and cut up big people food. Ma's voice, wistful over long distance, haunted me as how neglectful I had been. It was high time for a visit home. It took some doing to convince John that it wouldn't kill him to watch his sons for a few days during his Easter break. Bad driving weather arguments wouldn't wash. April had loosened winter's frosty grip and the roads were clear. As an enticement, I offered to also visit his parents and see his sister's twins. The sole announcement of their birth had come via Ma's grapevine talents. 'Uncle' John had to agree to somebody making a duty visit. Neither of us had known how to handle the Saddle silence, so to date had done nothing but mail two identical Carter's infant snap-crotch outfits. White, edged in pink. I stubbornly had not phoned because I thought it was up to John, son and brother to that family. John had assumed that wives automatically assumed responsibility of that sort. Unaware of his assumption, I had passed on that chore. John was persuaded that it was a good idea for me to visit his folks.

Taking total charge of a seven-month old baby he did not buy. Lizbet, who volunteered in the church nursery, who was familiar to

Little Ray, who certainly was used to baby care, and good at it from the contented look of Katrinka, offered to keep my baby for a few days in her own home. She intended to borrow a porto-crib from the church.

Sally and Jenny, the two teenagers who lived next door, displayed an almost frightening enthusiasm at being asked to spell John a few hours a day while I was gone. They had a crush on John, to them a tall, handsome, authority figure. I knew from past experience that their idea of babysitting was to insert a Disney video tape and watch it with an almost equal maturity as their charges. I knew that this diversion was growing thin. Benny and Bobby were so familiar with the Disney movies that they were able to mouth the dialogue with the cartoon characters in perfect lip-sync. So much the worse for the sitters if forced to behoove themselves to come up with more creative distractions. Surely their idol, the omniscient dean, could both handle and help out with that exigency. So much the worse for him if he couldn't. I shed a mother's over-protective skin and hit the road.

Long-range freeway driving frees up the mind for free-range thinking. As I headed back to the scene of the 'crime', Del held center stage in mental venue. Was the sperm 'theft' a crime, per se? What if Del had conceived? What were the ramifications? What if the lately-perfected DNA testing stood up in court and proved John was the father? Could he be judged responsible for child Support? The car's right-wheel radials scraped gravel on that angst-promoting supposition. Niccolo Machiavelli's motto got me back on the concrete track. The end did justify the means. At least sometimes. A baby would have made Del and her father ecstatic. I hummed along for two miles convinced that no harm had been done because no baby had resulted. Then I had to go and get another plaguey notion. Did I know for sure that no baby existed? For my own peace of mind I really needed to make contact with Del.

Associated, but less hair-raising thinking continued peripheral to the closer attention I had to pay to where I was going. A missed exit ramp meant miles of extra driving. Some good had come out of my association with a lesbian. First-hand education had broadened understanding. John Paul's attitude towards homosexuals had softened to accept Derek in friendship. A revision of his former views. He had a new respect for all the students in his drama class, particularly a talented young man named Harry. As I've said before, this hetero was no dab hand at picking up signals, if signals there were, on who might be gay, but Harry fit the stereotypical mannerisms abroad of how a gay acted. And I don't mean 'acting' as in drama class. He was quite frankly gay and didn't care who knew it. Bravo for Harry, cheered I. Why was it important, anyway, that the whole world be privy to anyone's private life? How disgusting that the genius mathematician Alan Turing had to sensationally bare his soul before a judge in a public court, and be sentenced to medicinal prescription drugs for his condition for which there was no cure. More than four decades ago, and still the ignorant in the land continue to bash gays. Murder them. Oops! So upset I almost missed my exit ramp.

On route 84, thoughts rerouted closer to home. How would I feel if one of my sons turned out to be homosexual? Brothers, yet they differed from each other in build, mental development areas, interests, moods and personality traits. Little Ray was content to watch his big brothers. Go with the flow. No flack. Introspective and patient. An expert wrote that a woman does not reach her optimum maternalism until she has a third baby. Hypocrite, me. I sincerely hoped that my experienced skill as a mother was the one and only reason for Little Ray being the gay little fellow he was.

In Willoughby, my parents were so happy to see me that they dashed out their front door onto the driveway as I pulled in. A bask in the lovelight shining from their eyes did me as the perfect welcome. They had their chick all to themselves, free from husnand and children, and they had my full attention. I certainly had theirs. We had returned to a time when we were a family unit unto ourselves. The chance to pamper me brought them no end of pleasure. Basically intact, my old room was familiar and unfamiliar. Ma had whomped up all the food favorites of yore. Many nutritionally unsound. I ate them anyway. A food splurge is soul-satisfying. However, a three-day fatladen spree was almost too much of an excellent thing. Who could complain? The visits included long soaks in the tub, Dick Francis' latest mystery among the books on the nightstand, and uninterrupted sleep, to sleep, to dream, until I chose to wake up. As if afraid to let me out of her sight, Ma insisted on coming everywhere that Vickie went. That was okay. Her talking a lot was okay, too.

I got a word in edgewise to ask if she minded if I looped around past the old house before we met Uncle Victor and Zelda for lunch..

"So why not, sweetheart? You do whatever you like."

The exterior looked the same, except the lawn patch had been manicured into flower beds that would bloom in the spring, bulb spears already pointing the way. A glimpse of the old backyard fence actually choked me up. No one was home. Good. For me,
I preferred not to see the interior decorator changes. I drove on quickly to gain the time to drop in on our real estate agent.

Claire was on the phone. She smiled recognition, held up an index finger, turned a palm up to indicate a please be seated. She had not handled the sale of Del's house. She knew who had. Gave the fellow agent a call. The friend had access to a computer, an up and coming tool on the cutting edge of marketing. The machine pulled up the data that Delilah Sealman had transferred the check received for the sale of her house, to a home savings and loan institution in Sherman Oaks, California. Sherman Oaks was almost the same thing a Los Angeles. Claire doubted that the Sherman Oaks bank would give out any information on a client. Long shot, or not, it was all I had, and I planned to phone, write, wheedle, and badger until maybe an address was forthcoming.

Ma, tired of waiting in the car, came forth into Claire's office.

"What is this business that is so important your mother is left sitting in the car?"

Claire, intuitive by profession, caught on at once. Extended her hand.
"So nice of you to bring your daughter to say hello!

Vickie was one of my favorite customers. What do you two have planned for today?"

Nice redirection. Ma fell for it. "We are supposed to be meeting my brother for lunch. I think already we are going to be late."

Zelda's tearoom had become a 'room'. It had spread out into the decorators' shop, into a sort of eat and decide nicety. It worked for me. Zelda had added coffee machines to her equipment. Derek dropped by in time for custard flans and espresso. Uncle Victor's beverage overflowed with whipped cream. Looking chronologically backwards, Zelda's place could have been the inspiration for the later 'Frasier' sitcom coffee shop scenes. Uncle Victor offered me a sip from his mug. Strong coffee with a milk chocolate undertaste. A closer inspection suggested a slight weight gain. How many of these did he drink per day?

No one gained entrance to Ma's kitchen domain. I gained cracks of free time while she tried to make me gain a pound or two. Ruth Rendell's 'Tree of Hands' was the last novel in the bedside stack. Thank goodness it had not been the first. Reading about a child's death due to a hospital's negligence gave me the creeps. A kidnapped replacement toddler blew my mind.

I had been away from my children too long. I couldn't sleep. I filled in the Plain Dealer crossword puzzle in a hyper seven minutes. Skimmed the fatter than ever newspaper. Tried not to think about the trees turned to pulp. Recycling was not in vogue then. Sought crises in the news to avoid thoughts of imaginary crises happening in Pennsylvania. Found one. A lesbian had professed her faith in the catholic religion and joined the church. Quote: "Life is not worth living unless I can include this part of myself (lesbianism), no more than it is worth living if I cannot profess my faith." The article said the young woman did not have a significant other. Okay. I guessed that the true test of her acceptance would come when a life partner came along. If she confessed to a sexual relationship with another woman, how then, oh pope of Rome?

Since that publication, the Roman church has released an about-face encyclical to advise parents of homosexual children to love those children. Did parents need permission to do this? I thought not. Having seen this light, I turned off the bedside light. I lay, eyes closed, thankful that John and I had joined a church that accepted everyone as all God's children. A visiting preacher, into the nineties, presented one of the best, and most applicable to daily life sermon, that I had ever heard. He wore an earring in his right ear. No confessions, no excuses, no stigma attached for any differences. All God's children.

Getting back to the early eighties. If I forced myself to fall asleep the time would pass more quickly until it was time to get up and go home. The Christmas Eve/Christmas morning theory. Vacations were great. Going home was the greatest. An intrinsic trade-off. My home was wherever John, Benny, Bobby, and Little Ray were. No longer where I was, but where I was going to go to.

## XXXII

I arrived home a success in finding out one recently changed address. News for John. The Saddles had moved. The migration had taken place so suddenly that Ma barely had gotten in a visit to drop off her handmade crib quilts and to take a squint into the matching bassinets. She said Paula and Philippa were as alike as two peas in a pod. Ma had been sworn to secrecy on the new address, but she didn't think the secret was to be kept from me. The Saddles had bought a horse farm in Virginia, and had moved themselves, plus Mary Jane and her two daughters, into a different life-style. Ma insisted that 'that stick of a girl' was sober and being a good mother. I hoped so. One fact for sure, Mary Jane had a kinship with animals, horses in particular, and was a professional level equestrienne. 'Saddle Farm'. Sorry, Will Shakespeare, what's in a name has been proven to have more to it than meets the eye—or the nose. People with odd first names often are oddball people, or so psychologists have discovered. How roses smell is a whole other story. Ma's story was that the Saddles had done a midnight flit to elude someone.

John had heard my story. He knew all about the move. His mother had called while I was away visiting. It was darned egodeflating to have the wind taken out of one's dispatch sails like that. Was there anything worse? Yes. Failure. The bank in Sherman Oaks had replied in the negative to my letter. The account in question had been closed. Their policy was not to give out personal information without a client's consent. Impossible in any event because the client in question had moved from the address in their files. A couple of unladylike expletives crossed my mind. Aloud, I settled for "Oh poop! and double poop!" Another dead end.

Little Ray held up his end by toilet training himself without formal training. I figured he did it either by osmosis or peer pressure example set by his brothers. Early. Before age two he was out of diapers. His accomplishment guaranteed his acceptance in the nursery school/daycare program. Which opened up an opportunity for me to have time to begin designing a course, Dietetics 101, to submit the next year for college level accreditation. The Board of Directors deemed it timely and worthy, and the following September, a month after Little Ray turned three, enough students had signed up for me to get a foot in the door of Academia. So what if they thought the course taught how to lose weight?

Our triplet mortgage holders knew about the board's approval before I did. Millicent, Tilleson, and Lilith still had direct pipeline info at their command. The congratulatory letter was postmarked Florida. Postcards arrived regularly from all over the world signed Milly, Tillie, Lilly. Victims of the same name diminution—ie—as my two older sons. I decided then and there to cancel the little in Ray's name. At three, he was as tall as Bobby and growing into a challenge for Benny.

Christmas break at the college released me from teaching my one course to set holiday preparations in motion. A husband who was likewise off duty, pitched in like the good sport he was. And the older his sons got, the better he interacted with them. He helped with the church Christmas pageant. They had parts in it. Shepherds in sacking. We threw a cheese and wine party in our decorated home. Company seemed an answer to fill in for the company we would not entertain from Ohio. The boys needed to celebrate Christmas in their own home. Ma and Pa feared winter driving. Virginia claimed another family branch. Uncle Victor and Zelda were booked on a Christmas cruise. Derek and Gordo? Who knew?

Benny, Bobby, and Ray refused to settle down on Christmas Eve. They were as strung up as the lights. Their parents were as unstrung as only pre-Christmas priority pressures could make them. On top of the energy drain, John seemed to be coming down with a head cold. At eleven p.m. he took two aspirin and took my advice to go to bed. At minutes to midnight the cowboys heeded an or else warning, either they stayed in their bunks or else no present opening until after lunch on Christmas Day. My best schoolteacher voice never failed. They knew I meant it. The lone survivor, it fell to me to haul out hidden packages for display around the tree, and to walk the dog. A snow no-show, instead unseasonably warm and damp. Soggy ground beneath Ruff-Ruff's wire run behind the house fostered an untethered run on the front lawn. The old cookie trick in my pocket would bring Ruff-Ruff to heel, as it had in the old peccadillo Del days. Ruff-Ruff wriggled and sniffed among the foundation plantings and went about his business in doggy fashion. I attended to the business of unloading the mailbox. No slot in this door. The postman deposited our letters in a black metal box with a sloping lid that was attached to the wall beside the front door. A half dozen greeting cards had arrived in time to be delivered before the year's most important day.

Santa Claus chores done, left me completely undone. A flop onto the parlor sofa, the better to behold my handiwork, brought to hand the envelopes I had tossed there. A sucker for unopened mail, this gal couldn't wait until morning. Five to Mr. and Mrs., one to Victorina Saddle. A tiny palm tree embossed the envelope's back flap. How inappropriate came to mind, until I thought tiredly, well the first Christmas was under palm trees, was it not? The card face wished the reader an 'Aloha Merry Christmas From Hawaii!'. Protected within its fold was a photograph. Grouped around a little girl about Ray's age posed Del, Les, and a man I guessed to be Del's father. On the photo's flip side: "We did it! Meet Victoria Leslie!"

Freeze frame. Time stood still. No eye blinks. I could do nothing but stare at the four smiling faces. Where had I seen that little girl before? My brain computed it to a black and white photograph in a sterling silver frame, an image of Mater Saddle when she had attended Infants School in England at the age of four. No DNA testing required. That little birl between Del and Les was Mrs. Saddle's granddaughter. My John's daughter.

Conscience click, click. What you dont' know won't hurt you? How believable was that asininity? Had I given away the very sperm with a plethora of 'X' chromosomes to produce a daughter for me? Upon what balance sheet did making three people happy at other people's expense work out evenly? Also, a newly-risen bete noire. Secrets leak out. Even Sperm donors may be revealed, no longer the right to remain incognito. On the Oprah show as a group so Victoria Leslie could meet her father for the first time? Teenagers ask a lot of questions. Mine do, so I know. Did I do right? Did I do wrong? Maybe both? Maybe not. But this never can be

## THE END

of it.